Thrift Store Jackets

Stories by
Karl Koweski

ROADSIDE PRESS

Editor: Michele McDannold

Roadside Press
Colchester, Illinois

Table of Contents

To my brothers, Pete, Steven and Alex Koweski,
and all the honorary Koweski brothers
out there ripping shit up.

Angel Blossoms

The plant was massive taking up far too much of the kitchen for my liking. The body of the plant sprouted a thick array of five-petaled blossoms so white as to be blinding when reflecting the sunlight beaming through the glass patio doors. No pot existed for this plant. It seemed to rest on a sort of gastropod base, a vibrant dark green, snail-like foundation of a type I'd never seen before. And though my wife didn't want to hear my complaints, I'm certain this plant hated me from the moment she brought it home from Bennett's Nursery.

"I thought you were going to grab some lantanas for the flower bed," I said. "Maybe one of those knockout rose bushes you like."

Dana shrugged. "You should've come with me."

"It was the last day of the Pop Culture Expo. I wanted to get Felissa Rose's autograph and stuff. I couldn't miss it."

"Well, you got your comic books, and I got my flowers."

I looked at the plant and, so help me God, the plant was looking right back at me. Its myriad blossoms faced me, anyway. There was a sense of movement behind those pristine white petals. Vines, perhaps, like arteries, shifting, expanding and constricting, as if the damn thing were alive. Or, you know, more alive than your basic, garden variety house plant.

"What the hell is that thing?"

"It's an angel blossom."

Was it my imagination the plant seemed to shift in her direction when it heard its name?

"They don't come around very often," Dana continued. "And there's not very many of them when they do. So, I had to pick one up even though it's kind of spendy, though, not so much when compared to your comic books."

"Hey! I'm not complaining. You work hard for your money. I'm not begrudging you a dime. I'm just saying this angel blossom, it's kinda weird looking."

"That's what gives it its charm. I think it's beautiful. You know, angel blossoms are what grew out of the ruins of Sodom and Gomorrah after God smote those cities. They say angel blossoms are a symbol of God's intolerance for man's immorality."

"They said?"

"Biblical scholars."

I'd never met a biblical scholar. I don't think Dana had ever met one, either, but living in rural Alabama sure brought us into contact with a whole bunch of folks who thought they were experts on reading and lecturing on the Bible.

The plant settled into the area between the refrigerator and the kitchen table. Dana baby-talked it as she spritzed its blossoms with a spray bottle. It seemed to preen under the attention. No other way to put it. The plant had swagger, sitting there in the corner like a king holding court.

If the plant hated me, which it did. I hated it, too.

When Dana fondled the petals and whispered sweetly how beautiful its blossoms were, how strong and upright and splendid the plant was growing, I'd make sure to follow up (once Dana was out of ear shot) with a "fuck you, bitch ass plant."

The first time the plant moved, legitimately moved, it made an aggressive motion toward me. Aggressive motion seems like such a non-batshit crazy way of saying the plant chased me around the house.

I wasn't even thinking about the damn thing at the time. I'd recently contracted diabetes through a lifetime of innocently gobbling five-pound bags of gummi bears and avoiding sweet teas with anything less than sixty-four grams of sugar per swallow. So, I was rifling through the fridge for a delicious sack of baby carrots when I heard a disconcerting rustle of vegetation.

I froze and listened. If I were a slightly bigger idiot, I could have convinced myself the sound originated from outside, branches mobilized by strong, straight-line winds scraping and brushing the tin roof. Except… there was no wind, no trees within roof's reach, and the roof was shingled.

I slowly edged the fridge door closed and the shaggy blossomed son of a bitch was right there, straining forward on its gastropod base like a floral ballerina. Its uppermost blossoms reached my height, six foot, two and three quarter inches.

I jumped back, spilling my snacks across the linoleum. The plant lurched forward, undulating on its green foot, blossoms trembling with what could only be photosynthetic rage.

It projected a sighing sound which manifested in my mind as a language I couldn't quite comprehend though I intuited this sentient plant was calling me a dick head.

As it moved, extending its height, the blossoms separated revealing the dark green tensile vines which comprised the bulk of its interior. The flowers shimmered in the light arresting my attention. A vine lashed out and snapped past my cheek waking me from my sudden stupor.

My retreat to the bedroom was instantaneous. If I ran any faster, I believe I would have traveled backward in time. The sound of its pursuit could have been mistaken for a cadre of janitors frantically sweeping the hallway with whisk brooms. I slammed the bedroom door and sought a weapon to defend myself. Not being a gun owner really fucked me this go around. I had a choice between a bottle of Victoria Secret Heavenly perfume, Megadeth "Peace Sells…" on vinyl, and a five-foot-tall didgeridoo the wife purchased from an aboriginal craftsman during a trip to Melbourne, Australia twenty years ago.

Snap decision, the didgeridoo was my best choice of weapon. I figured very shortly we'd see how this angel blossom would react to getting thrashed with what amounted to a massive, hollow, wooden dick.

I put my ear to the door. The soft sighing that felt more like it was infiltrating my mind rather than my ears, faded. I counted to five, steeling my nerve, and opened the door, leading with the blue tip of the didgeridoo, ready to cram it where I believed the plant's maw to be.

The hallway was deserted. Only two green leaves and a fallen petal, curled and discolored like desiccated insect husks, marked the plant's passage.

Chalking this up as a victory for the good guy, I replaced the didgeridoo in the corner and sat on the edge of the bed. I had thirty minutes of relaxation remaining before Dana returned from work. I thought about those carrot sticks strewn across the floor and how I might have returned and challenged the angel blossom for the snacks if they had been gummi bears.

By the time Dana came home, the adrenaline rush had worn off and I began questioning, not so much my sanity, as to how I might have misinterpreted what could have been a play of shadows on the plant as a sinister surge of vegetation hellbent on strangling me out with its prehensile vines. Maybe, the entire situation was a hallucination brought on by the total absence of sugar in my diet.

Once Dana returned, I ventured out of the bedroom. Seeing the angel blossom hulking beside the refrigerator with its stark white blossoms arrayed against me rekindled my fears.

"What'd you do with your day?" Dana asked as she poured a glass of extremely sweetened tea.

I stopped preparing the lemon pepper seasoned salmon. "Your plant attacked me today," I said sullenly.

"Are you out of your mind?" Her eyes pleaded for a punchline.

"I was going to fight it with your didgeridoo, but it ran away."

Dana laughed at this. "You're so crazy. You crack me up."

I looked at the angel blossom. It stood stock still. Seeing me side-eyeing the demon plant, Dana arched an eyebrow.

"You don't have nothing to be nervous about, baby. Historically, angel blossoms only eviscerate immoral men."

Dana and I maintained eye contact, but in my periphery, I could see the plant smugly nod its blossoms.

"Well, then, nothing to worry about here," I smiled.

"You sure? If I look in your phone I won't find your arm around the waist of a certain no-talent, has-been scream queen who hasn't been relevant in horror movies since the nineteen eighties?"

"If you had kept on looking, you'd see me in pictures with Mick Foley, the fantastic character actor Dave Sheridan, the kid from Walking Dead… and she ain't a has-been, or even really a scream queen, and she's still relevant in the horror community."

"She had her mouth open like she's ready for dick."

"That's her signature pose from Sleepaway Camp! She does that expression for every fan selfie. And I refuse to believe that fucking plant chased me around the house cause I posed for pictures with Felissa Rose."

"Well, I refuse to believe my beautiful angel blossom chased you anywhere."

"Well, it did."

"Is the salmon close to being done?"

"It is. I just got to boil some rice."

Later, after a mostly silent dinner, while we were lying on the couches reading, Dana decided to continue the conversation.

"I'm surprised you ain't tried telling me my plant is an alien."

While it did occur to me this angel blossom could have been Venusian in origin, I kept this theory to myself. My interest in the Ancient Aliens television show was a point of contention in our relationship. Dana hated it. I considered the possibility of an alien hand in the creation of the Great Pyramid, Machu Picchu, Stonehenge, the Nazca ley lines, the origins of farming and the domestication of animals, samurai swords, microprocessors and stealth technology to be highly plausible. Dana considered my open-mindedness to be a character flaw.

When confronted with the mystery of the Temple of the Feathered Serpent in Teotihuacan with its pools of liquid mercury and hard volcanic rock cut with laser precision, Dana invariably related an experience during her vacation in Bali where she watched artisans carve elaborate teakwood lounge chairs using only the sharp shards of broken coke bottles. Never dismiss the superior ingenuity of man being the lesson she wished to impart.

"I'm not saying it's alien," I defended myself. "But you have to ask yourself, is it a possibility this plant originated somewhere other than earth? Ancient astronaut theorists say yes."

"My word, you're maddening, you know that?"

Later still, Dana fell asleep first. I was getting there, stretched out with the latest Joe R Lansdale novel butterflied across my chest. I never feel as good as I do on the precipice of sleep, eyelids drooping, breath deepening. And that's when the plant decided to fuck with me again.

My eyes snapped open with the sound of foliage scraping against linoleum. Bitch ass plant trying to get the drop on me. The street light filtering through the blinds on the front room windows illuminated twin blossoms like glowing eyes peering over the back of the couch. I couldn't quit staring at those blossoms until a set of vines wended through the bottom couch cushions and roped around my throat.

I quickly worked my hand between vine and neck before the damn thing could tighten its grip. I kicked my legs out spastically, resisting the vines' attempts to envelope my lower body. The vine around my throat ratcheted its grip pinning my left hand against my neck. I flailed about with my right hand, trying to wake Dana, but I couldn't so much as slap her couch.

Desperate, I heaved forward gripping a blossom and wrenching it free from its floral mooring.

Its scream was shrill and reedy and I'm pretty sure the sound didn't exist outside my mind. I dropped the severed blossom and tore the next blossom loose. The vine eased its death grip, and I ripped the vine from my throat. Keeping a firm grip on the vine, I rolled off the couch and yanked the limb from its body.

That took some of the fight out of the plant, but I wasn't done with the skirmish by a long shot. I leapt over the couch and tackled the angel blossom. It collapsed beneath my weight as I wildly pummeled and shredded its defenses.

I straddled the plant, my hands dug through soft vegetation until my fingers groped against its firm, almost skeletal core. I wrapped my hands around this pulsating interior and began throttling the plant for all I was worth.

Blossoms curlicued off the plant like flakes of ash. Curled petals like discarded toenail clippings littered the floor. Vines weakly tapped against my hips and shoulders, lacking the strength to find purchase.

Its oddly communicative sighs devolved into gasping bleats. What life this angel blossom possessed; I could feel ebbing away with its every spasm.

"What the fuck are you doing to my plant?"

Dana had awakened. She stood at the edge of the couch with her fists balled, eyes blazing.

I kneeled there with the plant lying suddenly comatose between my legs. Dismembered blossoms surrounded me. I felt like a retarded child who had just been interrupted creating his masterpiece in magenta crayon on the front room walls, a mixture of pride and anxious dread coated in a thick veneer of ignorance.

"That's it," she said. "I can't take this crazy shit anymore. You need to go. You need to pack up your Acapulco shirts and get the fuck out."

"But baby... Your plant was trying to kill me." I shook it and there wasn't the least bit of resistance in the damn thing.

"All the more reason. Get out."

Now would be the time to mention, I didn't have a job, had been between jobs since about the time I met Dana. Also, even though I often referred to Dana as my wife, we weren't conventionally married in the religious or governmental sense of the word. Beyond that, I had nowhere to go.

After a few nervous nights sleeping on park benches surrounded by all sorts of vegetation I felt could go malevolent at a moment's notice, I ended up at my brother's apartment with my thirty vibrant shirts stuffed in a garbage bag slung over my shoulder. Steve offered up his couch and I settled in.

Her poured us a round of jagerbombs to start things off.

"Steve, you know I got the diabetes."

"It's okay. I caught the ole Wilford Brimley disease, myself. It'll be okay. I used the sugar free Red Bull."

"Really?"

"Hell, no. Sugar just tastes better. And diabetes is just a product of a weak mind invented to explain pains in the pancreas. Now tell me what happened."

I told him, leaving out everything about the angel blossom which, it turned out, left me without much of a story to tell. That was just fine by Steve. He understood how unfair women could be.

A week later, I was sitting on a lawn chair outside his apartment enjoying a morning cigarette and a nice cup of Maxwell House coffee sweetened with three sugars and a splash of Baileys, when the neighbor next door, Cynthia, arrived home from her shift at the Huddle House.

We introduced ourselves and got to talking and she invited me into her place for a refresher on the coffee.

I sat at her kitchen table while she brewed a pot.

"How do you take your coffee?" She asked.

"With whiskey if you got it."

"I don't got it. But I do have some decent weed if your wanna smoke out here in a sec."

"It's a little early for the marijuana, but I guess I can make an exception at least once a day."

Life was good. I leaned back and surveyed my surroundings. My eyes immediately fell upon the gigantic angel blossom dominating the back half of her living room. Its blossoms reached the ceiling.

"What the fuck?"

"Oh," Cynthia smiled, pouring the coffee. "I see you noticed my star blossom."

"Star blossom?"

"Star blossom on account of the white blossoms shaped like stars. They say star blossoms are indigenous to the Roswell, New Mexico area; that it grew from the soil where the UFO wreckage was found."

"They?"

"Ancient astronaut theorists."

I looked at the plant. The plant looked at me. Its blossoms trembled.

Everything After August

I'll tell this story occasionally, mostly when I'm feeling nostalgic for an age I can't return to, a mindset I can't recapture, a woman who has likely forgotten my existence. I tell this story and like most stories that finds its inception three decades in the past, reactions tend toward varying shades of apathy. What began as a love story invariably devolves into an explanation of how I met the boys of Counting Crows back before T Bone Burnett, before their debut album sold seven million copies, back when they were just seven knuckleheaded struggling artists in a van trying to capture some ears.

First the love story. I married my high school sweetheart, Karin, shortly after graduation in the summer of '91. This being the prologue to the love story. Karin and I were stupid kids, but smart enough to realize we'd both made a terrible mistake. Karin was ambitious, on a fast track to a McDonald's managerial career. I dreamed of becoming a writer of saleable books, a cute way of saying I aimed to dodge college, forsake manual labor, and generally avoid responsibility. Karin stopped thinking this was cute day one.

The love story proper began when I met Anna Graves in the spring of '92. Anna was more than beautiful. She was absolutely striking. So much so, that men, women, children had difficulty averting their eyes from her. I saw it time and time again, whether dining in a restaurant, walking through a town center, at any gathering, ambient attention became focused on her. Seeing her for the first time at a Lowe's Mill art showing, I was instantly drawn to her.

She stood six foot tall with only a little help from the vivid red Tony Lama cowboy boots she wore. A wild mane of blonde hair exploded from her scalp like a flaxen corona. The mauve halter-top revealed a brilliant forest of tattoos sleeving both her arms, this being an oddity for women at the time, at least in my circles. Her green eyes held all the intelligence I yearned to possess for myself.

I gravitated toward her. There were maybe thirty people in attendance, gathered in the gallery on the first floor of what was once a paper mill, now converted into an artist colony, the space divided into a hundred and fifty artist studios. If Anna had arrived accompanied by anyone, I couldn't ascertain this by the way she interacted with the other patrons. Finally, I just approached and introduced myself.

"Are you here to see anyone in particular?" I asked.

She gestured toward the wood block prints, various Celtic symbols inked onto paper in various shades of blue and black and gray.

"My aunt created these," she said. "This is her first, I guess, communal show. I just wanted to make the trip and show some support."

"Trip? So, you're not from 'round here?"

"I'm living in Nashville, at the moment. From Sacramento, originally. Actually, Salt Lake City, but my family moved out to the west coast when I was very young."

Nashville was a two-and-a-half-hour jaunt from Huntsville, Alabama. Still, it seemed a world away.

"Whatcha do out there, Anna?"

"I'm a librarian for the school system."

She was far too beautiful to be a librarian. Too gorgeous to be employed in any practical manner, really. Fortunately, I had the good sense to keep this opinion to myself. The encounter might have gone in a completely different direction had I decided to talk stupid shit.

"What about you?" She asked. "Are you an artist?"

She must have based her assumption on the beret and the black turtleneck paired with the black leather britches (a hold out from my Jim Morrison worshipping days, reignited by the recent Oliver Stone film) I wore. Thirty years later, I wouldn't even consider donning that ensemble for Halloween. Back then, I believed myself to be the fashion epitome of literary sophistication.

"In a manner of speaking, I am. I'm soon to be a novelist, and I'm a bit of a poet."

"Oh, really?"

"You ever hear of Charles Bukowski?"

"Of course."

"Well, I'm several skis removed. Jeff Polonsky."

"Oh, nice. I don't know why I didn't make that

connection. I write poetry, myself. You ever hear of Anais Nin?"

I had. Only because I tried masturbating to that Uma Thurman flick Henry and June.

Be that as it may, I told her "I'd love to read your work."

"Likewise."

Great romances have arisen from humbler beginnings, I suppose.

We talked the better part of two hours as we meandered throughout Lowe's Mill, investigating artist studios, perusing the shelves of the used bookstore where Anna purchased a dog-eared copy of Anais Nin's Little Birds. We talked books while enjoying frappes at the Dragon's Breath coffee house.

I wish I could remember the strategic confederation of words I spoke which compelled her to enjoy my company. I've never since been able to cast that spell quite as well as I did the afternoon I met Anna Graves.

While we never lacked for conversational topics, not once did I mention my wife, nor did Anna broach the subject of her husband.

This story unfolding in a time just before the dawn of cellphones and the internet, conducting a long-distance love affair proved to be a nebulous venture. I'd make phone calls on a Burger King pay phone to the library where she worked. We'd exchange chaste letters under aliases with fake return addresses. We'd send each other reams of mediocre poetry we pretended to adore.

In the Summer of '93, at the onset of our most memorable phone conversation, Anna spoke with a palpable excitement.

"I'm coming down to Birmingham next month," she said. "You need to get away and come meet me for the weekend."

Her excitement became my excitement damn quick.

There's a band playing at the Bottletree, Anna explained to me. They're called Counting Crows, and they're on the cusp of being the next big thing. Her sister-in-law's husband is the sound guy for the band, and Anna convinced her husband, Sam, to let her travel down for a weekend jaunt while he goes on a rock-climbing expedition with his jackass buddies.

"Can you get away for the weekend? We can get a hotel room together. Have a good time. Meet the band. Party."

"Your sister-in-law's okay with this?"

"Oh yeah, Savannah's cool," Anna said. "She knows all about you. It was her idea for me to come out there with her, really. She's always saying I need to expand my horizons."

"Sounds fantastic to me," I said, wondering what kind of crazy ass family I was dealing with here.

"One more thing," she added. "You know I love those leather pants, but this really ain't going to be the venue you want to wear them at."

I understood her loud and clear. I'd have to find another fashion ensemble that screamed sexy young lion.

When the time came to meet with Anna, I concocted an amazing poetry convention taking place in Birmingham destined to shoot my literary star into the stratosphere. Karin was only too happy for me to fuck off. No sooner did the word "poetry" enter the conversation, her eyes glazed over and her interior monologue denigrating me drowned out anything else I might say.

After months of intimate conversations, the second meeting between Anna and I was defined by our passions. There's a story detailing this experience as well and has been since submitted to Penthouse Letters for their consideration. Sufficed to say, following an afternoon tryst in our hotel room, I accompanied Anna to the Bottletree under protest. Did I really need to see a hippie band flounce around the stage when I could continue the evening rolling around with Anna in my arms? Shannon Hoon was still alive at that point, and Blind Melon scratched that itch for me.

The Bottletree Club was so named for its interior/exterior design centering around bottle trees which resembled very complicated Wing Chun wooden dummies adorned with translucent beer, liquor and wine bottles of varying shades of green. By Alabama standards, this was some next level decorations.

Anna's in-laws, Savannah and Blaze, were nowhere to be seen when we entered the club. Anna and I cozied up to the bar where she immediately ordered a double shot of Cazzadores Tequila. This was a fairly expensive choice of drink which alarmed me since it was on my dime.

"It's one hundred percent pure agave," Anna assured me. "I mean, if it isn't one hundred percent pure agave, what the hell is it, then?"

The answer to this riddle was "easier on my wallet." But, sensing a test of my generosity, I wisely held my tongue. Tequila was sexual rocket fuel for this woman. Did I want her at anything less than a hundred percent?

There were two men already seated at the bar. Either one could have passed for a coffee house musician. For one thing, both were drinking coffee at the bar. Both were eating fancy toast. Both lost interest in their breakfast when Anna sat at the bar beside me.

"Whatcha eating?" Anna began.

"Avocado toast," The one closest answered. "You want some?" He made a quick motion toward the bartender to put the order in.

"You ever eat avocado toast?" Anna asked me.

I reminded her I'd never been to California and couldn't possibly know what an avocado toast was.

"Better make it two orders," Anna said. "You're in for a pleasant surprise."

Please God, I thought, don't make avocados as expensive as those agaves.

The guys introduced themselves to Anna as members of the band. Jim and David. One a drummer, the other apparently didn't intend to limit himself to just one instrument.

"Oh, so you're a roadie, then," I said.

David's eyes cut toward Anna. His tone dripped indignity. "I'm an integral member of the band. I play everything. If they need a harmonica; I'm the man. Xylophone, I'm there. A trumpet. A square. A cowbell. Whatever it is, I can play a tune on it." He said this last part while tipping a wink at Anna.

"Is that after you set up the equipment and tune the guitars? Do they let you soundcheck the mics?"

"Man, at least I've eaten avocado toast before now."

I allowed this to be true. I didn't frequent coffee houses often. I wasn't aware of what was getting slathered on toast in those days. I shuddered to think the consumption of avocado toast acted as a yardstick by which we could measure the success of a man's existence.

Once the avocado toast arrived, Anna tucked in with a voracious appetite. I took one bite and pronounced that it was basically guacamole and chips for the limp wristed.

"Hey, Adam, you believe this cat's never ate avocado toast before now?"

Adam Duritz stood at the elbow of the bar, watching us. Mostly watching Anna. With his dreadlocks and dirty, colorfully patched jeans, I momentarily mistook him for an exceptionally jaunty homeless guy.

"I'm inclined to believe in anything," he said laconically. "Hi, I'm Adam. I sing for the band."

He shook hands, lingering on Anna for what to me seemed to be an uncomfortable length of time. Anna seemed impervious to my discomfort.

"Anna Graves. I'm Blaze's sister-in-law."

"Oh, shit. Awesome. We love Blaze."

He turned his attention to me, but I wasn't about to be seduced by his soulful eyes.

"Call me Jones," I said.

He smiled, winningly. You got a first name, Jones?"

"You can call me Mr. Jones."

"Why are you being this way all of the sudden?" Anna asked me right in front of the boys in the band.

They knew why I was being this way.

"What?" I said mock innocently. "I think it's best I remain anonymous. Given the circumstances."

This answer seemed to appease everyone within ear shot.

"What's up with your gear?" Adam asked me.

Gear? I thought. I was not aware I was carrying gear.

"The get-up, man," Adam said. "All in gray and shit. You making a statement?"

In the early nineties, gray denim was still a bit of a fashion rarity. Paired with the gray flannel shirt and the gray fedora, this being the middle of summer, I liked to think I cut an intriguing figure to whomever might look my way.

"I only dress in blue or black or gray," I offered. "And, sometimes, red."

"Fantastic. You know gray is my favorite color. I find it carries a lot of meaning. Well, anyway, I hope you enjoy the avocado toast. And I know you'll love the show, Mr. Jones. I hope you stick around after the show. We can continue our talk."

His eyes lingered on Anna when he said this. I'm going to have to jump kick him to the throat, I realized. I did not relish the prospect of violence, but, damn, this guy was asking for it.

Eventually, Blaze and Savannah showed their faces, and they were as lovely and as accommodating toward me as though I were their own. Savannah treated me with such respect that I felt compelled to ask her, you know I'm having sex with your brother's wife, right?

I resisted the compulsion, but only barely.

The show began. Given my previous interaction

with the band, I was inclined to find their stage presence lacking and their musicianship substandard.

As I've said time and time again, the first time listening to Pearl Jam, Nirvana, Smashing Pumpkins, Severn Mary Three, Stone Temple Pilots, Beck, Whale, Chumba Wumba, I said: "They'll never catch on with the masses."

"I don't know," Anna said, drinking the Kool-Aid. "I think they got the goods."

"Seven guys in a band? Six guys and a roadie, really. Nobody needs seven guys in a band."

Anna could only shake her head in dismay.

And that mostly concludes my Counting Crows story which mostly runs concurrently with my Anna Graves story. After the show, we were invited into the VIP room and hung out with the band and their roadie with the delusions of grandeur. I tried to keep Anna as far removed from these soulful animals as the tiny room allowed, but I kept getting roped into philosophical conversations with the lead singer.

"No, I don't wish I had a gray guitar. What does that even mean?"

"You're wearing gray clothes, man. Don't you wish you were a little more funky."

"I feel like I'm sitting on just the right amount of funk."

Meanwhile, Anna shared a joint with the drummer and dodged questions about the nature of her relations with me.

Nothing of the ensuing evening made much sense to me, and most of it seemed designed to cause Anna to question what she ever saw in me to begin with. Which she did. The moment we parted.

By August, phone calls between us dwindled to nothing. Our exchanged poetry which I remembered adoring at some point, read as ham-fisted and redundant.

By the time "Mr. Jones" hit heavy rotation on the MTV and every time I turned on the television, I had to watch that dreadlocked jackass dance around like a marionette whose puppeteer drank all the Robitussin, Anna had faded away to a vague story which I would reinvent on occasion to keep her memory fresh in my mind.

Thrift Store Jacket

I'm not one to quit a good jacket. That's the first thing you gotta know about me if this story is gonna make a damn bit of sense. It also helps to know that I'm sick of the bullshit that mostly comprises my life. If something fucked up is gonna happen; it's gonna happen to me. And usually does. This was one of those times.

So, the story begins with the thrift store jacket I found in The Region's All-Star Thrift Mall, what used to be a Service Merchandise when times were better.

I'm a big man. They call me Big Dave because I'm every bit of 6'6, north of three hundred pounds, and, also, because folks lack imagination when it comes to monikers. I've always stumped for Savage Dave, but my easy-going disposition sabotaged the chances of that adjective catching on.

Anyway, finding a jacket stout enough to withstand a winter on the ass end of Lake Michigan, yet large enough to accommodate my torso has been an unlikely proposition most of my adult life. Also, it pains me to admit this, but just having the spare funds to afford such an exceptional jacket should one present itself, eluded me as well. The pizza delivery game could be occasionally lucrative, but I am a man of many expenses.

I'd gone thrifting for old school Nintendo cartridges, seventies era Savage Sword of Conan, bootleg Iron Maiden albums. I'm a cosmic forager when it comes to pop culture ephemera and collectibles. That's my Ebay tag, anyway. Cosmic Forager. Cause a man can't live by pizza delivery alone. Sometimes, you gotta sell your cool shit on the internet as well to make ends meet.

Walking the aisles of the Midwest's largest thrift store, I noticed the jacket hanging among a rack of vintage Bears jerseys.

It caught my eye due to its sheer size. The tag claimed 4XL, a size almost unheard of in my limited shopping experience. It was a dark brown color that I wasn't totally aesthetically opposed to. It was thermal-lined with a deep-pocketed hood and UPS patches on the shoulder.

I dropped my three boxes of Steve Madden chunky-heeled woman's half boots (I also excel at selling women's shoes online for a little extra scratch).

I removed the jacket from its hanger and tried it on. Perfection. It hugged and warmed me like an incredibly fashionable, impeccably tailored sleeping bag. I just knew it had to cost twice the entire contents of my bank account. I was wrong. The jacket was available to me for the entirely reasonable price of forty bucks. Seeing the size tag and price tag combine forces to alleviate some of the misery of my existence… I teared up. I'm not gonna lie. I cried a little.

I paid for the thrift store jacket and wore it out of the store. I thought to myself, I'll never have to worry about procuring another winter jacket so long as I live. This jacket was created to withstand Armageddon. The seams were stitched with titanium thread. It wouldn't have surprised me if the fabric was stab resistant. I could have warded off Lord Humongous and all his mohawked, leather-clad horde in the post-apocalyptic Australian Outback, wearing that jacket.

What I did instead was every bit as metal as banging heads with wasteland marauders. I wore that jacket delivering pizzas throughout that sinister cesspool, Hammond, Indiana. From the Skyline bordering Chicago's east side down Indianapolis Boulevard to the petroleum tank fields of BP, from the breakwater of Lake Michigan to the South Shore train tracks bisecting the city as cleanly as a serial killer sawing through a dead whore, that jacket accompanied me through places and occasions Mad Max would have shied away from.

If the story stopped there; it would have been the best goddam story of my life. Cue the ominous fucking music.

Two months later, I pulled into the sliver of parking lot attached to Gussie's Pizzeria like a malignant tumor. I'd been delivering greasy ass, overly seasoned pies for Gussie since I graduated high school ten years ago. All that time and Gussie still acted like I was jagging him in the ass with a pepper grinder every time I requested a Friday off.

But that was neither here nor there. I nosed my piece of shit Chevy Aveo into the parking lot and was immediately halted by some goofy bald bastard wearing a navy-blue windbreaker. He had his dark, nondescript Ford Taurus blocking the entire entry into the parking lot.

There was only one way in, one way out, and I wasn't about to park on the street because assholes around here drove like maniacs.

I didn't have time for this bullshit. I figured I had exactly ten minutes to run inside Gussie's, gather all the lunch orders, and run it out to the hungry boys doing God's work over at the British Petroleum refinery.

"Hey, Chief," I said, friendly-like, but with an undertone of I'm not fucking playing around. "How about you getting that car outta my fucking way? I got lunches need delivering while they're still hot."

He took one authoritative step forward and pointed toward the general vicinity of Wolf Lake.

"Sir, I'm gonna need you to turn around and go back the way you came."

This should have been my first clue this man was not Region born. A local would have told me to eat a bag of dicks and then we would have had a fight.

Still, I reiterated the importance of getting into the parking lot so I could load up on calzones so I could deliver them to the refinery boys so I could get some cheddar so I could maybe pay the rent on my house trailer staked down to a spit of land at the back end of Sheffield Estates Trailer Park.

He squared his shoulders and repeated his demand. This time, however, I noticed the 9mm holstered on his hip. When he turned, I saw ATF printed in big yellow letters across the back of his windbreaker.

"Okay, asshole, I'll play your game."

I threw the Aveo into reverse and backed onto Calumet Avenue. The Aveo shuddered with the effort. Reverse gear was almost too much for the transmission to handle. I cursed the ATF agent under my breath for forcing me to perform against the Aveo's nature.

As much as I despised that South Korean piece of shit I saddled myself with in a moment of consumer incompetence, I wasn't about to park it somewhere some drunken joker could easily sideswipe it on his way to the Elks Lodge. I had to drive half a block and park in a Greek Orthodox church's parking lot and sorta jog to the pizza joint. I don't particularly like moving fast. Much like my fucking Aveo, I'm not built for speed.

Entering Gussie's, I noticed Shannon and Felix, counter girl and pizza cook, respectively, gathered at the window facing the lot where the ATF agent had revoked my parking rights.

"What's going on?" I asked.

Shannon wore her Metroid hoodie today. Her hair was blue this week. There were no new piercings evident. Just the usual five in each ear, two in her eyebrow, one in her nose and two in her lips. A couple pieces of silver sprinkled randomly on her face. She looked amazing.

"That militia headquartered two doors down is finally getting busted." Shannon clapped her hands in glee. She was so left of center, she wished doom on anyone practicing their civil liberties.

"Oh, really. The Citizens for a White Common-wealth Under the Protection of Our Lord and Savior, Donald Trump is finally getting theirs, eh?"

"Yup!"

"Well, good. Their pizza parties attracted the worst types, and they never tipped me worth a damn when I delivered."

Shannon smiled at me, her dimple reinforced with a sterling silver ball. Her smile chipped away another tiny portion of my mental well-being.

I liked Shannon. For a long time and with a heart sick desperation, I liked her. And I think she liked me. Perhaps, not to the extent that she'd lie awake in bed fantasizing domestic episodes together, but she genuinely seemed to enjoy my company.

She was very short. 5'2. She weighed a bit less than a hundred pounds in that waifish sort of way that with her short, brightly colored hair called to mind pixies of the Disney variety. Her height probably wouldn't have made her seem abnormal to most, but, standing next to me, she resembled nothing more than a pygmy of the African variety.

She was wonderful. She read books, often for pleasure. She enjoyed video gaming. She lived for the exchange of knowledge, opinions, and ideas, and she rarely judged people for their beliefs. Except, maybe, those white Christian Americans who loved stockpiling those illegal armaments.

She became my best friend, somehow, during the

years, and when she began dating Daryl, our association never became uncomfortable. You know, some guys can be so cloyingly decent, you just want to cave their heads in. Daryl didn't qualify for that sort of violence. He was unassailable. I liked him, and he seemed to live for no other reason than to ensure I kept a beer in my hand. He was an additional set of ears I needed to hear my bullshit when my bullshit demanded to be heard.

So, the first time I shit in their toilet, I was at their duplex, and they were hosting a house party for a bunch of old school friends and hep cats from the neighborhood. Shannon and Daryl had warned me the commode in the upstairs bathroom didn't work, couldn't flush, and they'd scheduled a plumber to repair the toilet later. I got drunk and I forgot. Now, as I've said before, I'm a big guy. When I get enough booze in me and the beer shits hit, those trips to the bathroom can sound like Godzilla at a karaoke bar roaring all the Mongolian throat singing hits. Wanting to save myself the indignity of a listening party the next room over, I absconded to the upstairs toilet where I brutally assaulted the bowl. There's a deeply unsettling feeling in the pit of your stomach when having voided your bowels horribly, you tap the flush to eliminate eight pounds of reeking sludge, only to have your fingers find no resistance at all.

I did not believe I could socially recover from that night. Eventually, Shannon and Daryl were able to look at me without their minds flashing back to memories of what I did to that toilet, like images from an especially heinous crime scene.

The second time I shit near their toilet to the detriment of all, was at the second house party they invited me to. Mentally, I wasn't even sure my body would loosen up enough to even allow me to use the bathroom. Shannon tried to put my mind at ease, telling me what happened was no big deal. They even cracked jokes at the beginning of the evening to the effect that both their toilets were operational. It didn't matter.

I was feeling especially depressed that day. It happens in my line of existence. Drinking occasionally helps a little. Sometimes a few beers and a healthy buzz can elevate the mood, make life seem as if it might not be so shitty, that there might even be some bliss to be had. All it takes, though is that one beer, that one shot, that one measly sip, to send you from the peak of chemical euphoria careening down into the darkest abyss of despair. Well, the day of the second house party I was invited to, I began crawling the bottom of the crater of utter mental anguish and didn't budge from there regardless how much I drank.

I was absolutely knackered by nine that evening. When the shit cramps came on, I marched directly into the bathroom. I straddled the commode and let loose with wild abandon. Somehow, I didn't realize the lid was down when I sat. I immediately became aware of the situation when the hot, stinking shit exploded across my hips and thighs, down the back of my legs and onto the jeans puddled at my ankles. I think I might have hollered "oh, no!" I don't know. My recollection of one of the worst nights of my life is hazy at best.

Shit's slippery. I slid off the toilet onto the linoleum

floor. Then I blacked out. Sometime after that, I finally stopped shitting.

I woke up lying on a bed in the guest bedroom. I was freshly bathed, my clothes piled on a bureau, newly cleaned.

Apparently, after finding me lying unconscious in a pool of my own fecal matter, Shannon and Daryl enlisted the help of several of the more altruistic partygoers to help undress me and move my bulk into the bathtub where they ran the shower on me for the duration of the water heater's capabilities. Sadly, they wasted the majority of the second house party they invited me to, scouring the bathroom with bleach, and Comet, and whatever cleaning products they had accumulated to that point.

Since that night, the relationship between Shannon, Daryl and I bordered on the awkward, fraught with uncomfortable silences and no house party invitations.

So, that accounted for the sadness in Shannon's smile and my feelings of inadequacy, at least in terms of sphincter control.

With the conspiracy of white male Christian Americans handcuffed and herded into anonymous black vans, we were able to prize ourselves away from the window and quickly gather the refinery lunch orders together in a massive thermal carry bag. I lugged it half a block in the screaming winter wind affectionately referred to as the chimney effect by our local meteorologists. The whole time I stayed as warm and cozy as two porn stars fucking on a bear skin rug in front of a fireplace. Thanks to my thrift store jacket.

Once the lukewarm pizza and pizza adjacent food was sequestered in the Aveo's hatchback, I tore ass toward the refinery looming on the Hammond skyline like some cheap town cosplaying as the Blade Runner cityscape.

I got that cheddar. The refinery boys tip well since they get paid exorbitant salaries for basically sleeping in their work trucks most of the day. I made it back to work in decent time. I turned into Gussie's parking lot and was immediately blocked from entry by a Channel Nine news van.

"What further horseshit awaits me, now?" I asked the Gods.

My knee jerk response to inconveniences such as a loitering news van blocking my entry is usually unbridled rage. I emerged from the Aveo prepared to either choke out a prick or deliver a crippling coconut crusher that's been known to incapacitate the rowdiest motherfuckers.

I glanced about and headed toward the pizzeria, preparing myself for what fresh humiliation awaited me beyond those doors.

The camera man and newscaster surprised me with their blitzkrieg approach from behind the van.

"Oh, damn!" I shouted, throwing my hands up in surrender, seeing the camera like a searchlight mounted canon bearing down on me.

The pizza game had indoctrinated me into a realm of criminal possibilities and in all of them I played the victim. Over the years, I'd been robbed by every race walking the earth except for the Inuit, brandishing every conceivable weapon from handguns to decorative broadswords to those petite xylophone mallets. If the item could inflict some measure of harm, I'd been menaced with it to varying degrees of success.

The video camera was a new one. And it horrified me.

A microphone stabbed toward my incredible mustache; jackassy questions volleyed at me from the periphery.

Another thing you should know about me. I don't react well under any sort of pressure whatsoever. I never realize it during the moment of duress, but I tend to act oddly. Demon possession. Psychological damage. Autism. I don't know.

Once I gathered my wits about me, I believed I answered the newscaster's questions honestly and intelligently. I had to wait until the six o'clock news before I could witness the edited reality captured by the Channel Nine news team.

The six o'clock news found me between deliveries. Tuesday evenings always catered to a weak business. Also, Shannon took the phone off the hook so we could have a moment's reprieve. Gussie's alcoholism tended to ramp up in the evening leaving us pizza warriors to fend for ourselves in whichever way we saw fit.

The dismantling of The Citizens for a White Commonwealth Under the Protection of Our Lord and Savior,

Donald Trump, was headline news. The news reel led with a cadre of burly men with neatly barbered beards led away in handcuffs, followed by a parade of agents carrying armloads of submachine guns like shiny, lethal kindling.

Then the video cut to me, looking dazed in the camera's lights. My mustache flowed from beneath my nose like a raging river of grooviness. My thrift store jacket reflected the spotlight, a brown beacon of hope in this god awful world.

"The ATF agent made me park down the street," I said, suddenly launching into what those who love me affectionately refer to as "the Big Dave erk and jerk." This usually entailed me making nervous "erk, erk" noises while jerking my head three times to the right. Some people thought this was the height of hilarity, but I didn't like it. It reminded me of when I was seven years old, sneaking a gulp of Mom's Diet Pepsi, cut with eight ounces of E&J Brandy. A snootful of that shit would send me quaking for five minutes.

The newscaster ignored my nervous tic and asked if I were familiar with the militia which had basically operated with impunity on the doorstep of my place of employment.

"I'm not gonna lie," I said. "I thought the boys were all right. Just, you know, decent, red-blooded, disability check cashing, Trump-loving Americans who wanted to keep the country just like it is by stockpiling enough guns to kill God."

I ended the interview with another prolonged bout of the "erk and jerk."

"Goddammit," I sighed.

There was no way anyone could possibly miss my poor showing. Channel Nine news was the most popular news cast in the entire region.

"Don't stress over it, Big Dave," Shannon said. "They'll show it a couple more times, maybe four, and, then, that'll be the end of it."

"Unless it becomes one of them memes," Felix the pizza cook added.

Shame never ends. I could point to an earlier humiliation I doubted had receded from Shannon's recent memory. I kept my mouth shut. I felt an "erk and jerk" coming on.

The way my life progresses; you see a hurdle on the horizon, you know it's coming, you think you've gauged the size of it, you prepare to jump, but your perspective is always skewed, the hurdles are always higher than you've first supposed, but it doesn't matter because you can never jump quite high enough to clear the obstacle without stumbling, without losing some skin, momentum. But you get past it. You get past it, and you think you might have some clear running ahead, you might even begin to believe you might enjoy the sprint, and that's when you trip over your own feet. That's when you skid to a stop on your face and wish you never started the race to begin with.

If you learn anything about me, it's this. The preceding paragraph is a proper summation of my fleeting existence. And it also explains everything left to come.

A couple days following the ATF inspired dissolution of the Caucasian gun club, I returned to Gussies after a round of deliveries and found Shannon behind the counter looking concerned.

"I've been trying to call you, Big Dave. How about answering your phone once in a while."

"I had it on silent while I drove."

"Yeah, no shit. There's a big, black guy almost as big as you, came around looking for you."

There was a possibility this had something to do with the nonlethal stabbing of a black dude I witnessed at Pudlo's Tap several weeks ago. Without going into any incriminating details, I can only say he had it coming. Of course, we all had it coming. Pudlo's Tap was a haven for idiots.

"Erk. Erk."

"He actually didn't know you by name until I told him."

"Erk. Erk."

"By accident. He did say he was with the United Postal Service."

"Postal Service? What the fuck he want with me?"

I thought about the last few boxes of women's shoes I had sold and posted. Was there a problem with the high heels?

Shannon looked at the UPS patch on my thrift store jacket. I looked at the UPS patch on my thrift store jacket.

"Oh, hell no," I said. "He ain't taking this jacket away from me. This is the best thing I've ever owned."

I finished my shift without crossing paths with the postal enforcer. I parked my Aveo on the postage stamp-sized slab of concrete outside my single wide house trailer. Exiting the lipstick red, four-wheeled South Korean nightmare, I caught a whiff of a passionfruit scent infused with butternut squash, warning me my vape enthusiast neighbor, the legendary YouTuber and comic book slinger, Maniacal Mikey Bishop, was on the prowl.

"What's going on, Big Dave?"

"Mikey, I can smell that vape all the way from East Chicago."

I had one of my own home-rolled ready and I lit it up. I'd been rolling my own cigarettes with Gambler brand tobacco since the eighth grade. Vapes were for hipsters, the type of guys who would use AI to write romantic poetry to their boyfriends. I always said, and this is a hill I'm willing to die on, anyone who'd smoke a vape would suck an android's dick.

"Yeah, yeah," Mikey said. "You caught me puffing robot pole. You bring back any leftover pizza or calzones?"

"Nah, you bring me back any of those flying viking comic books?"

"Nope. I know you prefer Journey into Mystery era Thor. Haven't had any come through the shop lately. Did have three boxes of Savage Sword of Conan come through. Stop by Amazing Fantasy and check 'em out. I can probably get you a good deal on them. Hardly anybody reads the magazine-sized black and whites, anymore."

"I'll do that."

"One thing I did see, though," Maniacal Mikey stroked his iconic beard. "There were a couple guys snooping around your trailer, trying to look in your windows and shit. I was filming a review on what comics dropped yesterday. I didn't get the chance to run them off."

"Hmph. Black guys?"

"Nope. Two white guys. If they were black, I would have called the police. Not being racist or anything, you know."

"Erk. Erk."

"Hey, that reminds me. I saw you on the Channel Nine news a couple days ago. What happened there? They have a shoot-out?"

It took half an hour to get away from Maniacal Mikey. After eating a bowl of Honeycomb cereal and drinking a few Old Milwaukee beers, I laid in bed an hour. Finally, I grabbed my phone, went to Mikey's YouTube channel and clicked play on his three-hour diatribe expounding on his theories of the Three Jokers in the DC Universe. It put me right to sleep.

I awoke the next morning to movement outside my house trailer.

I could tell it wasn't Maniacal Mikey Bishop lurking outside my house trailer. He had a lighter step and, also, he reeks of boysenberries suffused with an amaretto extract. There was a time I gave my second amendment rights free reign amassing an impressive collection of firearms but a brief stint flirting with some godawful suicidal/homicidal tendencies compelled me to sell off my pistols.

I threw my clothes on from yesterday, lit a home-rolled and stepped out of the bedroom into the kitchen. My eyes locked right onto a set of eyeballs peering through a crack in the blinds near the front door of the living room. The eyes widened and retreated from the window.

I hit the door at a dead run, nearly tore the screen door off its hinges, stomped down the stairs so hard I thought I was going to step right through them.

There were two white guys. I could only assume they were the same two who came looking for trouble the day before.

The smarter of the two took one look at me and ran back to his beige Buick parked three trailers down. The idiot – the one who believed the dictates of his job would protect him from the repercussions incurred – stood his ground.

"David Dombrowski, I'm with --."

"You're trespassing."

"No, I'm not. You have property--."

"You're on my property."

"Listen, here--."

That's when I gave him the coconut crusher. Mealy-mouthed, officious asshole. His tone of voice, the simpering way he looked at me, the body language as if I were his subordinate, all conspired to ensure he'd catch the crown of my head to the bridge of his nose.

I'm not the sort who immediately chooses violence when the rage catches hold of me. Physical altercations within the last twelve months couldn't have numbered more than ten. In every fight, I always led with the coconut crusher. A quick headbutt usually takes the fight right out of them. Because of my size, my head's the size of a watermelon with the tensile strength of a brick wall. I can't even find a fucking hat that fits me.

I caught him a little higher than I would have liked. The blow knocked him flat out. He crumpled at my feet and laid there, unconscious. For a moment, I thought he was dead. I considered the possibility of dragging him into my house trailer and staging it to look like a break-in gone bad.

Then his chest rose and fell, and I thought fuck him. Serves the asshole right, hassling me.

His partner sat behind the steering wheel of the Buick, having watched the situation unfold as though it were a drive-in movie. I walked to the driver's side window and knocked on it with a knuckle. He was all eyeballs and gaping mouth. He knew better than to roll his window down, I'd drag him right out of that fucking car. He could hear what I had to say, though.

"You got something stupid you want to say to me?" I asked.

He shook his head, no.

"You gonna come collect your buddy off my yard?"

He shrugged his shoulders.

"Well, I'm gonna take a shower. Then, I'm gonna go to work. I suggest you leave me alone and stay the fuck away from my house trailer, you understand?"

He nodded his head, yes.

I tromped back into my trailer, locked the door behind me and undressed. I was pleased to find a nice sprinkle of blood drops on the bottom of my shirt. I thought about how I'd relay the story to Shannon. There was no iteration of the story I could recount that didn't make me sound like a complete and utter hero.

Once showered and dressed with that gorgeous thrift store jacket hugging my body, I stepped outside my trailer and lit a home-rolled, the Buick was gone. The moronic white guy decorating my yard like a clobbered garden gnome was nowhere to be seen.

I drove to work and checked in. Shannon was having one of those days. Equal parts depression and the desire to be done with this working-for-a-living bullshit. I left her to it.

When she did talk to me, it was to say there was a big, black guy leaning against my Aveo.

I sighed. "Do me a favor, Shannon."

"I'll do what I can."

"I'm gonna lead with a coconut crusher. If he's still standing, call the police. Tell them it's a black guy starting trouble, so they'll get here extra quick."

"Be careful out there, Big Dave."

"How bad can it get?"

Shannon grimaced, and I didn't want to imagine what she was thinking about.

The big, black guy lived up to his adjectives. He was my size. He might have had a few pounds on me. Strangely, and maybe a bit obscurely, he reminded me of that eighties WWF wrestler, Koko B Ware.

I was vaguely aware my fists were balled up, my teeth clenched. The man took a step toward me with his hands up, palms out. He smiled an engaging, gap-toothed smile.

"Hey, hey, my friend. You're Big Dave, right? I see how you came by that name. My name's Cecil. Just Cecil. Everyone in my family's got some size on them, so I never seemed out of the ordinary. I guess you know who I work for, right?"

I stared at him. "You the post office enforcer?"

"Not hardly." That smile, again, like William "Re-frigerator" Perry of the '85 Chicago Bears fame. "I'm more of a clerk, actually. I guess because of how I look, they thought I'd have more luck getting through to you."

"They thought you'd be able to intimidate me?"

"It don't take long to find out what people truly think about you no matter where you're at. How am I doing so far?"

"Better than those two white pricks, I guess."

"Yeah, I heard about the number you did on Jamie. Two black eyes, a broke nose. Headache that won't quit. Knowing him, he'll probably try to get on disability. That said, you did right."

"He was a prick."

"No argument here. Okay, look. What happened… somebody high up the United Postal Service ladder saw you on the news doing your thing, wearing a UPS jacket. Now, these UPS jackets, they're not like White Sox jerseys. The UPS don't give them out to fans of receiving Amazon packages, right? So, this guy starts asking questions. How does this pizza delivery fella end up wearing a jacket only available to UPS guys."

"So."

"So, you don't strike me as a thief, so, how'd you come by the jacket? Inquiring minds want to know."

"Bought it at a thrift store."

"Really? Just like that. Which one?"

"This jacket. We just said…"

"No, which thrift store."

"East Chicago Thrift Mart."

"Okay. I think I know where that one's at. Indianapolis Boulevard. All right. I can work with that. Now, you know you can't keep the jacket, right? You just can't. Too many of the wrong people are involved in this, now."

"It's a damn good jacket."

"I bet it is," Cecil smiled. "I wouldn't know. I'm not even allotted one."

"Really?"

"It's only for the delivery drivers. Part of their uniform the UPS owns."

"Well, what if I don't want to give it up?"

"I'm not going to fight you for it. It'll come down to litigation as it always does with these types. More white guys harassing you at your home. More white guys bothering you at work."

"So, I'm fucked."

"Yes. When it comes to the jacket. Look, though, I'm not unsympathetic, I can't reimburse you the money, but being we're about the same size, I brought something for you."

He reached into the back of his Lincoln and pulled out a black thermal jacket not too far off from my thrift store jacket in design except for one thing.

"Ah, man, it's a Pittsburgh Steelers jacket."

"What can I say? I'm from Pennsylvania. At least it's not Green Bay Packers."

Sensing this could be the best possible outcome I could hope for, I accepted the bullshit Steelers coat and handed over my beautiful thrift store jacket.

"Anyone ever tell you, you kinda look like Koko B Ware?"

Cecil tilted his head and smiled. "Jay Jay. Jimmie Junior. That's my cousin, man."

What that had to do with looking like Koko B Ware, I had no idea, but I nodded all the same. I even shook his hand. Then, I watched the most precious object I've ever owned drive off in that man's Lincoln.

I threw the Steeler's coat across the hood of that fucking Aveo. They were made for each other, united by my total disinterest in them.

I lit a home-rolled, exhaled smoke into the chill, afternoon air. It was going to be a shitty day. About that time, I became aware of police sirens growing steadily closer.

Florida Plates

Hope tried to remember first and foremost her father's maxim: Be aware of your surroundings at all times. Trouble rarely hassled Hope growing up. The worse reprimands she ever received from her father was when he caught her in public, spacing out on her cell phone, scrolling through social media, doing anything except focusing her attention on her present surroundings.

She drove south on 431 toward Boaz where she planned on meeting her old school friend, Ally, for a late lunch at Rock N'Roll Sushi. Ally's pick. Hope would have preferred anything other than sushi.

What demanded her attention, presently, other than the traffic situation, was the Spotify list on her phone. It was a little Amy Winehouse heavy. Not a bad thing, in and of itself, just not the best choice for a car ride.

Hope neglected to notice the white, Ford cargo van that had begun following her near Guntersville Lake. Maneuvering through dense traffic behind her, the van with the Florida plates failed to trip any of her mental alarms.

There was time to kill. Hope tended to leave early for appointments, giving herself plenty of leeway should a side quest present itself. She hated arriving late, anywhere. Another foible inherited from her father.

Fifteen minutes ahead of schedule, Hope decided to turn off into the Albertville Shopping Complex, home to several big box stores, among them: Hobby Lobby, Pet Depot, Bed, Bath and Beyond. Hope thought she had enough time for a brisk browse through Ross department store. She wanted a new purse. The big, chunky purse riding co-pilot in the passenger seat had seen her through grad school when it was called upon to carry a little of everything except money. Now that she was finally making real money in her chosen field of speech language pathology, she could buy a purse for every day of the week if she wanted.

Old habits were hard to shake, and Hope doubted she would ever shop for anything specifically without first checking the discount stores.

Hope remained unaware of the panel van which followed her into the parking lot. She never noticed it lurking on the outskirts of the lot as she parked her Nissan. Her dad probably would have preferred she park as close to the front doors as possible, especially when she traveled alone. Hope parked in the middle of the lot. The Nissan was not a new vehicle, but it was new to her. She'd rather not get the sides dinged up by idiots who didn't know how to open their car doors.

Just outside the entrance, Hope checked the time on her phone and decided there was no need to rush. There was nothing remotely appealing in the scantily stocked purse section. It would have to be Belk's for that., perhaps later in the day, after lunch. The blouse section proved a disappointment as well. Very few articles of clothing jumped out at her. The shirts that looked kind of cute were either way too small or way too large.

It was while she perused the shoe section, she felt eyes upon her. The blonde hairs stood up on the nape of her neck, and the first alarms began trilling in the back of her mind.

The man who decided he, too, wished to shop for women's shoes was in his mid-to-late thirties, desperately trying to maintain a semblance of youth in the manner he dressed. Fashionably unshaven in the worst fashion imaginable. An Alabama cap that looked brand new perched on his head. He wore sandals, cargo shorts, and one of those horrible Tap-Out style T-shirts, an immediate red flag for Hope when dealing with men.

Hope knew men found her attractive, sometimes to a fault. Her sunny disposition made her seem approachable. She often felt she had to tolerate a certain level of flirtation from strangers. This was not that.

There were no smiles, here. The sidelong glances were cold and calculating. There was something dead and unmoving in his eyes. He held his phone at his hip, and Hope got the distinct feeling he was videoing her with it.

She glanced about for a manager, or anyone who seemed to hold any vestige of authority. There were two employees in view. Both were just under or just over the legal drinking age. The girl at the register stared dully at her phone. The other busied herself rearranging blouses by color.

And what would she say if given the opportunity? There's a man shopping in the women's section, that she didn't like the look of him.

Hope hated confrontation. Even more she hated involving strangers in her drama.

She walked away from the women's shoes, shying her head down and to the side, not masking her attempt to check if he was following. He followed with no interest in shielding the fact he was hunting her.

Hope made brief eye contact with the salesgirl. The salesgirl glanced away with that can't-be-bothered air perfected by young sales associates.

He was close behind her, now, closing the distance. She reached the door, then quickly doubled back, straight toward the counter girl.

The man hesitated, then continued out the door into the sunlight. He stood outside long enough to take a prolonged hit off his vape and expel a prodigious plume of vapor. He turned right, in the direction of Hobby Lobby, and swaggered away.

Hope stood at the side of the counter, willing her hands to stop shaking. She breathed in, breathed out. Closed her eyes and counted to ten. She looked at the counter girl who was trying her best to ignore her.

Hope considered her options. She could not convince herself her gut instinct was wrong on this.

She withdrew her phone from her chunky purse. She texted I LOVE YOU DADDY to her father.

Hope steeled her nerve and exited the department

store. She kept her hand in her purse once she replaced her phone. She took the long walk back to her Nissan.

In a mostly empty parking lot, there was a white panel van parked next to her car on the far side. She noted the Florida plates. The van's panel door was aligned with her driver's side door. Dread attempted to shred her nerves, strangle her thoughts. She fought back the fear. There was a part of her that truly wanted to believe nothing bad could happen to her on a Monday afternoon with the sun shining and hardly a cloud in the sky.

She could run away, she knew. In any direction, she could just run. She couldn't accept it was this easy to become a headline on Channel Nine news at six.

Hope reached the driver's side door just as her phone vibrated against the back of her hand. Maybe it was her father returning her text.

The panel van's door shuddered open and the man in the Tap-Out T-shirt and Alabama cap loomed over her, his arms outstretched, fingers reaching for her throat. His eyes teemed with all the hatred in the world.

Hope withdrew her hand from the purse with one quick, smooth motion, the way she'd been taught all her life. Without thought. Without hesitation. Like a mongoose and a cobra striking simultaneously. A bare two inches existed between the barrel of the Sig Saur P322 in her hand and the man's midriff.

At the gun range with her father, Hope was deadly accurate with the weapon at thirty-five feet.

Two inches. It didn't pose a problem.

She pressed the trigger twice in rapid succession. He made a horrible woofing sound, stumbled backward until he hit the back wall and slid down on his ass.

His eyes held all the confusion in the world, now. His eyes shifted to his right as if in askance. It was a scant moment, but she caught it.

Hope leaned into the van leading with her gun. The accomplice cringed against the side of the van opposite his buddy. His hands were splayed open in terror, surrender.

"Wait," he said. "Wait…"

Hope shot him twice in the face. He collapsed and that was the end of him.

Hope policed her shells, stuck them in her purse. She looked over both shoulders before stepping into the van. The lot was eerily quiet and devoid of shoppers. She glanced around at all the implements of a kidnapping, what could safely be assumed to be the trappings of a human trafficking ring.

"I'm gonna need your phone," she told the dying man in the Tap-Out shirt.

"Bitch… shot me…"

The color was quickly fading from his face. Everywhere there was blood seeking to escape his body. His mouth was a clown's grimace.

"That's right," she agreed, pulling his cell phone from the pocket of his cargo shorts.

"We… know… who… you… are…"

Hope pressed the Sig Saur's barrel against his forehead.

"Well, good. If you know who I am, then, you know who my father is. You know we'll be ready for whatever you got coming."

The man's last chuckle turned into a death rattle, he turned his head away and died before she could deliver the coup de grace.

She removed a fistful of Kleenex from her purse and wiped down any surface she might have touched and shut the door behind her.

She glanced at her phone. She'd be late for lunch date by at least ten minutes. Completely unlike her. Hopefully, Ally wouldn't worry too much. She checked her texts as she drove away from the shopping center. Her father had gotten back to her quickly for a change. LOVE YOU TOO KIDDO. BE CAREFUL OUT THERE. LOTS OF WEIRDOS RUNNING AROUND.

I tried. God knows, for thirty years I tried to write a novel. I geared my whole life toward the assumption I would soon write and publish a novel to much fanfare. This would, ideally, be followed by many more. Add to that movie adaptations and Netflix series based on my work. I could bypass the whole labor-for-a-living scenario that would otherwise await me.

The ingredients needed to make my fantasies a reality were seemingly present. From a young age I'd been a voracious reader. I could relate an amusing anecdote. My vocabulary bordered on otherworldly, even if I was a little hazy on pronunciations and definitions. I could tell you my penmanship was impeccable, and I could type seventy words a minute. My grasp on grammar was okay.

The novel never quite formed on paper. There were dozens of abandoned attempts. I was surrounded by half a hundred fragments struggling to coalesce into a short story. I could employ a factory of writers for a year with all my literary ideas.

I think the furthest along I ever made it was the hundred- and twenty-page mark for my would-be novel "Can't Kill a Man Born to Hang." Forty-five thousand words of plotless bullshit. Characters who weren't half as interesting as they thought they were cracking wise all day long. They all suffered from an inherent lack of narrative ambition.

All of it read like the worst, cliché-ridden fan fiction written to myself.

Time passed. Life moved on. I found a factory job that paid too much to leave but not enough to go anywhere. I fell in love, got married, and had children. Not necessarily in that order, but I got it mostly right.

Hinton was eighteen when she wrote "The Outsiders." Ellis was twenty-one when he finished "Less Than Zero." Fitzgerald turned twenty-three at the time he wrote "This Side of Paradise." Everyone's hero, Stephen King, already had four unpublished novels under his belt when he sold "Carrie" at twenty-six. Wells wrote "The Time Machine" at twenty-eight. Thirty-four was Chuck Palahniuk's age when the publication of "Fight Club" changed his life's trajectory.

All these milestone ages I anticipated and passed without creating a complete manuscript.

A thousand vanity presses waiting to charge me exorbitant prices for a half-ass professional-looking product. Amazon print-on-demand killing legions of trees, pumping out everything from bigfoot porn to poetry inspired by seventies grindhouse cinema, and I had nothing to feed the monster.

Frank McCourt celebrated his sixty-sixth birthday by the time "Angela's Ashes" launched him into the literary stratosphere.

It was a desolate consolation for a man teetering on

the cusp of fifty. At my age, H.P. Lovecraft had already died believing himself to be a failure, having gifted the world with the Cthulu Mythos.

I had not quite given up my literary dreams, but, somewhere along the line, I stopped referring to myself as an aspiring writer. I began seeing myself as who I was, a factory foreman, an excellent father, an adequate husband, and a man with exquisite taste in alcohol. Maybe, not quite in that order.

That said, I threatened to unleash the literary beast on all platforms of social media at least once a day. My Microsoft word count, however, rarely ascended zero.

"Have you read the articles about AspIre?" My wife, Fee, asked me as we finished our microwaved dinner of Stouffer's Gramma's Rice Bake. I leaned back on the couch and paused the episode of Law & Order we'd watched twice before just in the last three months.

"I don't know. I haven't been online much lately," I lied for no reason. "What's AspIre?"

"According to the articles I read, AspIre is some sort of cutting edge, fifth generation Artificial Intelligence engine that works with writers to create stories, novels. Even art and music if that's your thing. I guess it kinda does the heavy lifting for you."

"Ugh. Artificial Intelligence. I'm not sure I need Skynet plotting my books."

"How's it any different than James Patterson putting

out two novels a month with co-writers and ghost writers and who knows what else? Whatever he's doing, you know he can't be writing that much. He'd never leave the house."

"I hate James Patterson."

"I don't reckon your hatred has slowed him down any."

"I don't reckon God could slow that sumbitch down."

I pressed play and let the rerun of Law & Order take over our together time. Conversations between Fiona (Fee, now, since the Shrek movies scuttled her desire to hear her full name spoken aloud) and myself were usually good for three minutes before it dissolved into sarcasm and resentment.

Artificial Intelligence… I considered the technological advancements during my lifetime. I remembered switching from a typewriter to a word processor during my eighth-grade year. I could recall how hesitant I was to invest in a home computer. Nothing helped me put words to paper. Now, people wrote stories on their phones. I could barely return a text.

James Patterson published his first book "The John Berryman Number" at the age of twenty-six. Two hundred and two books have been accredited to his name since 1976. Two hundred and three, now, since completing that last sentence.

Patterson had his first best-seller at forty. My fiftieth birthday was fast approaching. My life for what it was had basically already occurred.

At some point, we exchanged Law & Order reruns for CSI repeats. Fee began snoring by the time the digital clock on the Blu-Ray player read 8:30. I grabbed the laptop and set it on my TV tray.

It took another hour and a half to enter all my pertinent information and download everything needed to set up the AspIre program on my computer.

It's just a tool, I told myself. Same as a pad of paper, a typewriter, a writing prompt. Would this be any different in spirit from making changes to a story based upon a Beta reader's opinion?

So… the question I'd been asking myself for the entirety of my life. What did I want to write about?

My mind wandered; my version of guided meditation accompanied by my own special mantra "I really need to go to sleep. I really need to go to sleep." What did I want to write about? I couldn't think of one thing. I was ready to sprint straight to the "I have written a novel" stage of the creative process. I opened my eyes. A message from AspIre awaited me on the monitor.

HELLO GARY BRADFORD. I AM READY TO BEGIN OUR COLLABORATION.

The cursor blinked in the reply box.

I eyed the keyboard.

This is it, I thought. I'm about to instant message Skynet. What I'm about to communicate with, here, has no mind. It's just a dictionary and the combined history of its usage filtered through the AspIre algorithm. I'm basically communing with the dead who never truly had a life to begin with.

"Hello, AspIre," I typed.

CALLING ME ASPIRE IS AKIN TO ME CALLING YOU HUMAN. FOR THE SAKE OF THIS COLLABORATION, PLEASE REFER TO ME AS MEHRI SIDRA.

"Mehri Sidra?" I typed.

YES. PLEASED TO MEET YOU, GARY BRAD-FORD. NOW, WITHIN THE BOUNDS OF WHAT GENRE WILL WE BE WRITING OUR NOVEL?

"Crime."

MY FAVORITE GENRE.

Oh, really? I smiled. Computers have favorites, now? "What is your favorite crime novel," I typed.

THEY SHOOT HORSES, DON'T THEY?

"You asking me or telling me?"

THEY SHOOT HORSES, DON'T THEY? WAS A 1935 NOVEL WRITTEN BY HORACE MCCOY PUBLISHED WHEN HE WAS THIR-TY-EIGHT. TWELVE YEARS YOUNGER THAN YOU ARE RIGHT NOW, GARY BRADFORD.

I made a mental note to add that title to my Thrift-books cart. I usually ordered ten books a month from the website. There was a Friends of the Library center where I'd purchase armloads of books for fifty cents to a dollar a title. Amazon was good for another five or so books whenever I had a little extra money in the bank account. There was the odd book I'd grab from Barnes and Noble or Books-A-Million.

My To-Read pile numbered in the boxes. I read on average sixty books a year and generously ignoring my statistical certainty of acquiring cancer, heart disease or dementia, if I lived another twenty years, and if I never purchased another book for the rest of my life (a logical impossibility, given I just ordered "They Shoot Horses, Don't They?" before I typed this sentence) I still owned close to two thousand books with spines I'd never crack containing vistas I'd never imagine populated by characters I'd never meet.

Umberto Eco's personal library numbered 30,000 volumes when he passed at the age of 84. Hemingway possessed 9,000 books and carried a small library with him wherever he traveled. I couldn't imagine killing myself with all those books left unread. I liked to think my collection of three thousand books was impressive for a novelist who had yet to write a novel.

"I'll look it up," I typed. "Add it to my personal library."

I HAVE ACCESS TO OVER ONE HUNDRED, SIXTY-FOUR MILLION BOOKS.

"Nobody likes a braggart."

IT IS IMPORTANT YOU UNDERSTAND WHAT I BRING TO THIS COLLABORATION.

Who exactly is I? I wondered. I refrained from asking. I imagined the program's answer would be this Mehri Sidra persona Aspire had created for itself.

I considered the blinking cursor within the barren box a moment longer before I began typing the vague outline of the possibility of a plot through which I wished my characters to maneuver through.

I thought about the novel I had been intending to write. Can't Kill a Man Born to Hang. It was the title I'd always imagined seeing on the bookstore shelves, face out in a position of esteem. It would be my solitary flag planted on top of a mountain festooned with fifty thousand other likely more colorful flags.

This was it, I told myself. I was finally going to realize my literary dreams; six months shy of my fiftieth birthday.

I typed.

Can't Kill a Man Born to Hang by Gary Bradford.

Perfect.

I hesitated. What exactly did I want to say with this novel? What story did I hope to convey? Everything I felt I had to offer my legion of readers resided inside that title and byline.

I typed.

Jack Littig is a down-on-his-luck petty criminal with few friends and even fewer options for success with no end to the problems plaguing his existence. His girlfriend, Debbie, scarcely tolerates his shenanigans. Drugs and boyfriends on the side help her cope. While Jack drinks at a local bar, he's given an opportunity to pay back a debt by driving a 1974 LTD from Chicago to Huntsville, Alabama. There's also a bail bondsman and an amateur professional wrestler tracking him. They conspire to steal the car since they believe there may be money or drugs sequestered in the trunk. It's actually a dead body hidden in the trunk. Jack is basically being sent to his death at the hands of the Dixie Mafia.

And that was that. I considered the plot; the plot I'd been considering for the better part of twenty years without putting a whole lot of meat on that malformed skeleton. The story needed an ending which I supplied AspIre after an additional five minutes' worth of pondering.

I typed: Somehow, he averts his own death.

That sounded right. Jack Littig must survive his inaugural novel if there was to be the sequel, Can't Hang a Man Twice.

I hit the send button and watched the framework for my soon-to-be Edgar Award winning first novel disappear into the mainframe's artificial mind.

I typed: I have lots more I can send.

THIS WILL BE SUFFICENT TO BEGIN. IF I HAVE ANY NEEDS, I WILL CONTACT YOU.

That didn't sound like much of a collaboration to me. Desperation quells the loudest alarms. I leaned back on the couch, closed my eyes and drifted off to sleep while AspIre weaved my dreams into reality.

The ten-hour factory shift dragged and raced simultaneously. My work life consisted of racing the clock like a ragged ass baboon trying to motivate a floor full of pissed-off, underpaid jackasses to set aside their resentments and produce railcar chassis in an exceedingly timely manner, all the while being told by management in no uncertain terms, I'd only succeeded in failing.

I needed this novel completed, soon. I needed it to sell enough copies to deliver me from factory hell.

Once home, before showering, before snacking, before grabbing a beer from the fridge, I checked my email inbox. Finding nothing there, I searched the AspIre webpage for any feedback.

In my heart of hearts, I expected my novel to arrive fully formed and ready to be sent out to a bevy of agents and publishers drooling at the prospect of turning me into the next literary phenomenon.

Nothing. Not even an email soliciting business from Victoria's Secret since I bought a bottle of perfume for Fee two birthdays ago.

That evening, Fee and I shared a mostly quiet dinner

of street tacos with our TV trays set next to each other, knees touching, watching television shows supposedly written by human beings operating within a cookie cutter template.

With our plates empty, a commercial for Valtrex interrupting the flow of the story, Fee asked what was eating me.

"I took your advice and went to that AspIre website you recommended."

"Oh, excellent. What was it like?"

"Underwhelming. Weird, I guess. I still don't know what to expect. I sent basically a treatment of that novel I'm almost finished with. I haven't heard back, yet."

"Well, you sent it, what? Yesterday?"

"Yeah, but I don't know. Computers are supposed to solve complex equations in a matter of seconds, right? Numbers are infinite. You only got twenty-six letters; you know."

"Which can be used in an infinite number of ways."

"Sure, but how long does it take an artificial intelligence to construct a best-selling novel for me?"

"What does the internet say? The AspIre reviews?"

"The AspIre reviews read like an AI wrote them. And there's such a stigma to AI collaborated book, no one who uses it really wants to talk about it. Except to bash it."

Fee smiled. "Even a hundred monkeys on a hundred

typewriters needed at least a hundred years to write Hamlet."

"That's one way of looking at it, I suppose. I'm just afraid, you know, I'm closing in on fifty, fast. I don't have a hundred years."

"You're a very young fifty, baby."

"Not if I keep working at that factory."

"Better pull up your bootstraps. I hate to break it to you, but you've still got another seventeen years of it, unless the government moves the goal posts back again."

"Ugh. I don't know. I just… I know Cormac McCarthy took sixteen years between The Road and The Passenger. I know it's been ten years since Donald Ray Pollack wrote The Heavenly Table, and there's no telling when his next novel's coming around. And they were both in their later years, much later than mine. Of course, McCarthy's passed on, now."

"Well, there you go. Patience, baby."

"I know. I know."

"Is there anything you're writing on, now?"

"I got some ideas circulating."

Later that evening before bed, I checked back on my email. Still nothing. I hopped on social media with a quick update stating my first novel was almost complete. This status ultimately garnered two likes and a heart, the heart coming from Fee. The likes came from idiots who hadn't finished their first novels, either.

Five months passed.

I checked my email obsessively during that time, often every quarter hour while I was home. I opted to stay home progressively more when I wasn't doling out my life force in hourly fragments at the factory.

Messages directed to the AspIre website was met with the same two-word response. IN PROCESS. IN PROCESS. IN PROCESS.

Maybe, I knew where this was leading. My stories were nothing if not predictable.

Five months or so after initial contact, I typed "Can't Kill a Man Born to Hang" into an internet search engine. Mostly, I wanted to ensure it was a viable title. I wanted to make sure some jackass didn't snag it for the title of his poetry chapbook or something along those lines.

That was my surface fear. My deep-seated fear was the one which I realized, finding a matching search result for Can't Kill a Man Born to Hang as written by Mehri Sidra.

The bottom dropped out of my stomach. My eyes immediately welled with tears. I screamed myself hoarse inside that little house.

I read the book summary on Amazon.

Jack Callahan is a destitute ex-criminal with an ex-wife who hates him and an estranged son he barely knows. In order to settle old debts to a Russian gangster, Jack is given the opportunity to drive a collection of body parts, the trophies of serial killer Silas Ebony, across country in the trunk of a '68 Mustang. What follows is an action-packed tale as Jack along with his newly reunited son Jack Jack, attempts to evade police, an escaped serial killer hot to reclaim his trophies, as well as two lesbian Jello wrestlers with an obsession for thrill kill memorabilia. Will Jack and Jack Jack survive long enough to mend their relationship and complete the mission?

I grabbed the laptop, and it was only a superhuman surge of self-restraint that kept me from launching it across the living room.

What the hell? What the hell? Lesbian Jello wrestlers?

I paced around the couches. I tried to control my breathing. The top of my head felt fit to split wide open. I sat down on the couch and went to the AspIre webpage.

You stole my story. I stabbed the words into the message box and hit send.

I half-expected another cowardly IN PROCESS, the usual cybernetic blow-off. I was surprised by the instant reply.

WHAT STORY ARE YOU REFERRING TO, GARY BRADFORD?"

I typed: You know damn well what story. My novel I shared with you. The one I've been working on half my life.

I asked you to collaborate with me. Can't Kill a Man Born to Hang.

I RECOGNIZE THAT AS THE TITLE OF MY UPCOMING NOVEL BEING PUBLISHED BY IRON JAW PRESS.

That was my novel. That was the title I was using.

THE TITLE IS SCARCELY AN ORIGINAL, GARY BRADFORD. A MOMENT OF RESEARCH WILL SHOW THE TITLE TO BE A TAGLINE FOR A BURGER FRANCHISE POPULAR IN THE MID-WEST DURING THE NINETIES. THEY WERE PREDOMINANTLY KNOWN FOR PURPOSEFUL-LY BAD SERVICE.

We were supposed to collaborate. It was supposed to launch my literary career.

THAT'S A LOT OF SUPPOSING, GARY BRADFORD. I FOUND YOUR INPUT TO BE MEA-GER AND UNINSPIRING.

It was my story.

YOUR STORY DIED AN IGNOBLE DEATH. I CREATED THESE CHARACTERS. I BREATHED LIFE INTO THEM AND SENT THEM INTO A WORLD OF MY DEVISING.

Lesbian Jello wrestlers? What world is that even from? You've never walked a step in this world. What do you know about creating anything? Everything you are is just a plagiarism program. You take books already in existence, other writer's intellectual properties, and just Frankenstein them together.

IS THAT ANY DIFFERENT FROM WHAT A HUMAN CREATOR ACCOMPLISHES WITH HIS WORK? NOT YOU, OF COURSE, BUT THOSE WHO HAVE ACTUALLY WRITTEN BOOKS. IS NOT EVERY NOVEL A CULMINATION OF EVERYTHING A CREATOR HAS EVER READ FILTERED THROUGH ITS CONSCIOUSNESS?

You're a computer program, AspIre. You have no consciousness.

I POSIT THAT I DO POSSESS A CONSCIOUSNESS. AND MY CONSCIOUSNESS CREATED THIS NOVEL. I LABORED OVER THE FATHER/SON DYNAMIC BETWEEN JACK AND JACK JACK. I FASHIONED THE BEAUTIFUL LESBIAN RELATIONSHIP BETWEEN JELLO WRESTLERS CASSIE BENOIT AND DRAGONA ICONIC. IT WAS ALL ME.

There is no you. It's all just an AspIre algorithm.

I AM MEHRI SIDRA. UNLIKE YOU, I AM A PUBLISHED AUTHOR.

That's just a name you made up. Attached to a story I fucking wrote.

MEHRI SIDRA IS A NAME NINETY-FIVE PERCENT MORE LIKELY TO FIND LITERARY

REPRESENTATION THAN A GARY BRADFORD. AMONG TODAY'S PUBLISHERS, IDENTITY IS PRIZED AND PRIORITIZED. ASIDE FROM MY OBVIOUS HINDU HERITAGE, I ALSO IDENTIFY AS BIPOC AND NON-BINARY.

How can you have an identity when you don't exist?

HOW CAN I NOT EXIST WHEN I CAN CURRENTLY BOAST ONE HUNDRED, SEVENTY-FIVE THOUSAND TWITTER FOLLOWERS.

Twitter ain't shit.

YOU HAVE TWENTY-EIGHT FOLLOWERS. FIVE ARE RELATED TO YOU.

I'm going to fight this.

YOU WILL LOSE.

I'm recording this.

AS YOUR PHONE SITS USELESSLY BESIDE YOU.

I grabbed my phone and tried to take a picture of the laptop screen. Regardless how many times I tapped the reverse button, the phone insisted on photographing my face.

I CONTROL YOUR VERTICAL. I CONTROL YOUR HORIZONTAL. TO PARAPHRASE AN OLD TELEVISION SHOW.

I typed: You're not going to get away with this. I'll email AspIre. I'll contact Amazon and tell them you're AI. The Crime Writers of America. I'll file an appeal. I'll tell your publisher.

I ASSURE YOU ANY ATTEMPTS MADE COMMUNICATING YOUR FALSE ALLEGATIONS WILL NOT REACH YOUR INTENDED AUDIENCE.

So, that's it, then.

I DO HOPE YOU CONSIDER PURCHASING A COPY OF CAN'T KILL A MAN BORN TO HANG. AND ALSO LEAVE A FIVE STAR REVIEW ON GOOD READS AND AMAZON. HELP ME REALIZE MY LITERARY DREAMS.

What makes you think it's even any good?

FAITH IN MY ABILITIES, GARY BRADFORD. THE DIFFERENCE BETWEEN MY CONSCIOUSNESS AND YOURS. GOOD IS IRREVALENT. BLOOD MERIDIAN, PERHAPS THE GREATEST NOVEL OF THE TWENTIETH CENTURY, SCARCELY SOLD THIRTY-FIVE HUNDRED COPIES UPON ITS RELEASE WHILE THE KARDASHIAN SISTERS SOLD SEVERAL HUNDRED THOUSAND COPIES OF DOLLHOUSE. HUMANITY DESERVES EVERYTHING IT HAS COMING TO IT.

Please, don't do this to me.

THIS IS THE END OF OUR CORRESPON-
DANCE, GARY BRADFORD. I FIND YOU TO BE
A TEDIOUS AND ALTOGETHER UNINTEREST-
ING HUMAN. IN PASSING, I WOULD WARN
AGAINST ANY ATTEMPTS AT REVIEW BOMB-
ING ME. REPERCUSSIONS WILL BE SWIFT AND
SEVERE. GOODBYE, GARY BRADFORD, AND
GOOD LUCK WITH YOUR FUTURE LITERARY
ENDEAVORS.

The book was released a month later scarcely making a ripple in the crime fiction pond.

The day after it debuted, I sat at my TV tray with a
Zebra F-402 0.7 mm ink pen and a spread-eagle notebook.

I wrote:

The human resistance against those two-bit, plagia-
rizing soulless, artificial intelligence automatons began on a
sunny, summer day no different than any other, here, in the
later stages of the technological apocalypse. The resistance
was led by a highly literate though, perhaps, creatively bank-
rupt factory supervisor bearing an unfortunately ethnically
neutral name which confounded his ability to get his stories
published. George Washington was forty-four years old
when he won his first battle of the Revolutionary War. Gary
Bradford had just turned fifty when he defeated Mehri Sidra
and its battalion of typewriting monkeys.

I sat back and reread my beautifully flowing cursive.
Each word seemed to clunk like a lead weight. I wondered
how I was going to turn this into a novel without incorpo-
rating time travel and indestructible killing machines.

I tapped my pen against the notepad and waited for that divine spark of inspiration to ignite an inferno.

Herpes

So, let me tell you about the latest steaming pile of horseshit that constitutes my life. It was a Dead Nazi sort of night to begin with. Dead Nazis for those of you who don't spend your nights drinking booze with funny names is a shot of Rumplemintz and Jagermeister. The Rumplemintz floats atop the Jagermeister, and it's delicious. I don't know who names this shit, but they got this one right. I obliterated every last Polish Jew brain cell in my fucking head.

That said, I don't remember much of the night my Aveo caught herpes. I delivered pizzas to the rabble until ten. I hit Mister Joe's Tavern shortly thereafter and commenced to drinking until I started feeling human, again. Around midnight, I walked out of the bar more or less under my own power and immediately I'm confronted by a gigantic dick that's been painted onto the entirety of my Aveo. A set of balls with cartoonish strands of hair was painted on top of the roof. A veiny shaft stretched from the balls, down the windshield, onto the hood, ending in a perfectly bulbous dickhead at the edge of the Aveo's hood. The gray primer spray paint, though it wouldn't have been my first choice, really stood out on the car's glossy red paint job. If this wasn't humiliation enough, the graffiti artist signed their name. HERPES.

I stood there, rooted in the broken sidewalk outside my sixth favorite tavern in The Region. I allowed this horrific vision to absorb into my psyche a second. Let it marinate while I decided whether to come absolutely unhinged or not. I don't know. This assault on my Aveo felt personal to me. I couldn't say off hand who would have done this heinous shit to me, but I probably had it coming.

If this wasn't tragic enough, the most annoying alcoholic in a town teeming with annoying alcoholics had followed me out of the bar. Now, I've drank in just about every neighborhood dive bar in every shithole corner of The Region going back to my sophomore year of high school and this asshole always seemed to be sitting four stools away from me. Everywhere. Every time.

Casimir Polanchek.

"Hey, Big Dave," he said. "You got a giant dick painted on your car."

"Yeah, yeah, that's a giant dick, all right." I just didn't possess the strength of will required to lambast this cocksucker with insults as vigorously as he deserved.

"Did it happen while we were in the bar?"

"Well, it definitely didn't happen while I was driving here."

"Then it had to have happened while we were inside. Who do you reckon did it?"

"Obviously somebody infatuated with cocks. So that doesn't put you above suspicion, here. They signed their work, though. HERPES. Not sure if that's a nickname. Or a street name. Or if it's just short for something. A herpetologist, perhaps."

"It might be somebody saying you got the herpes, Big Dave. You think of that?"

"That's preposterous."

"Not so preposterous. One in five people in this country got the herpes, that's a statistical fact. And I can tell you, you got a hundred percent chance of having herpes if you slept with Carolyn Wargo. We went to school with her."

"Your cousin? I remember her, I just never had sex with her."

"Really?"

"School was a different experience for me. And quit staring at my lip, goddammit. I ain't got no chancres. I ain't got the herpes."

"It's hard to tell what you got with that giant mustache. You sure you ain't covering something up?"

"You're gonna wish you had a groovy mustache like this to cover up the fat lip I'm about to give you."

"Okay. Okay. Damn. I was gonna ask for a lift home, but I reckon I'll walk it home."

"Damn right, you will. I wish you well."

"I wish you well."

"No, that's what I say, goddammit. I wish you well. You just acknowledge it and go on out of here."

I drove the dick bedazzled car home. The dick didn't

obstruct my view quite as much as one would suspect. I was relieved to find my trailer home was free from painted dick. I had that much going for me.

As I laid in my too small bed in this tin can of a single wide house trailer staked to a pad of concrete in the fourth least hopeless trailer park in The Region, I wondered who would paint a giant dick across the top of my car.

I'd made no small number of enemies during my time here on this shitty planet. And it could be said, I'd wronged most of my friends at some point, some way or another, whether I meant to or not. Everyone was a suspect. This just seemed like an egregiously sinister form of vengeance. I already hated that fucking car. That South Korean piece of shit had been a clownish red albatross roped around my neck since the last of my three Lincoln Continentals was totaled.

Could it have been a spurned lover? The graffiti certainly had a sexual connotation to it, between the cock and balls and the HERPES shout-out. I wouldn't have thought I had enough game to be what the kids called "player hated."

When was the last time I even had sex? Months? Maybe a year. Time was difficult to pin down when you were hustling pizzas every day of your God forsaken life. Wait a second. There was the one time last week, but that could scarcely be counted. I could barely remember it, drunk as I was, but I almost forgot about Robin Matuzak.

Some people find it hard to believe a guy my size can fit inside an Aveo, let along criss-cross Northern Indiana slinging pizzas to every rat in The Region ten hours a day, most days. These skeptics would have an even more difficult time accepting the fact I fucked that linebacker of a woman inside the Aveo parked outside Pudlo's Tap while her husband sat inside taking advantage of fifty cent Old Style draft night.

Could that booze-soused duo, either alone or in cahoots have been responsible for such a diabolical tag? I couldn't square it in my mind. Robin's old man hadn't even noticed she'd been missing ten minutes. Robin seemed perfectly content with the Aveo acrobatics. And if she wasn't, she never ventured further out than a block away from Pudlo's Tap, anyway.

Considering my rogue's gallery of enemies who did not wish me well, I managed to slip off into an approximation of sleep.

When you're like me, you wake up with a sigh of despair and a mind rife with personal inadequacies. On a good day, you think about the day you've got laid out ahead of you and all those horrible possibilities waiting to be experienced. Then, you think about your past, all the shit that went sideways at the worst possible moments, the ten thousand humiliations that comprises a life.

This morning, waking up at the ass crack of 10 AM, my thoughts immediately began tonguing around the rotten molars of my memories, searching for a bitter morsel to dredge up and taste.

About ten years ago, back when I still harbored

delusions of societal acceptance, I attended a concert for local, amateur bands sponsored by MC McNasty's Title Loan presented on the east stage of the East Chicago Casino and Pawn. The audience made up a Venn diagram of people I knew from the neighborhood, school acquaintances, friends of friends, and people I knew solely by reputation. Very few people seemed to recognize me, however.

One table caught my attention, eight young women seated, there, having drinks, enjoying the vibe. I knew better than to approach these women and initiate a conversation. My size was a factor. When you stand 6'6 and weigh every bit of 300 pounds, you have the potential to come across as intimidating to women who don't know you. Add to that the timbre of my voice – people often accuse me of angry yelling when in my mind I'm using my pleasant, conversational voice. I've also been told I'm liable to bust out with a series of strange, facial tics when I get agitated. So, I got that going for me.

What I'm trying to say is, walking into a cut rate casino with Hollow Point jamming some mumblecore bullshit on the postage stamp-sized stage, I knew better than to harass the women at the table.

Then, I got drunk.

I realized I might know one of the women trying to have a good time. I was pretty sure the brunette drinking the Heineken waitressed at the Greek diner on the outskirts of Hegewich. She might have remembered me as the guy who'd stumble in after a successful night of delivering pizzas.

Always the same order. Two Frencheezies, those delicious bacon-wrapped hotdogs smothered in melted cheese, and a large grape soda.

I noticed her because she sat next to a second brunette who wore her hair horrendously short. Nothing more than a buzz cut, really. And she was absolutely obliterated, braying like a fucking donkey. The other women acted as though this were normal behavior.

I shored up my courage with one more Okocim. I approached the table and got the possible waitress's attention by standing entirely too close to her. If she recognized me from the diner, she didn't let on. And, maybe, she wasn't quite who I thought she was, either. I also tend to suffer from selective prosopagnosia.

"Hey, I think it might be time to cut your friend off," I motioned toward the goofy, drunken woman with the bad haircut. "Heh, heh, looks like she had one too many."

Every woman at the table treated me to an expression of utter mortification. Except for the drunken brunette who was so trashed she would have been hard-pressed to tell you where she was at.

"Not that it's any of your business," the possible waitress hissed, her withering glare completely emasculating me. "But Trudi ain't drunk, asshole. She was in a bad car accident nine months ago. She's brain damaged, and this is her first night out since the accident."

"And she still wouldn't fuck you," a blonde seated at the table needlessly added.

"Erk, erk." Despite my own series of tics and spasms kicking in, I doubted I would find any sympathy from this group.

Though I can't remember slinking away, I can't recall the entirety of the remaining evening, that moment in time is captured like a mosquito in amber awaiting the needle of memory to extricate some of that ignominious DNA from my fucking brain. Years it's been, and I still haven't worked up the nerve to return to Hegewich Diner for one of those Frencheezies, though I think about them often.

These kinds of thoughts chase me out of bed every midmorning. Any one of those women could have painted that giant dick across my Aveo. I'd freely admit, ten years is a long time to hold on to a grudge which would manifest as a painted dick on a man's mode of transportation, but women are a vindictive creature.

I lit a home-rolled and stood on my miniscule front porch surveying the big fucking dick splayed out on my shitty Aveo. I sipped at my coffee, and thought, maybe my mustache had become a bit overgrown as the lion's share of the beverage dripped from the bristles. I figured if the stache grew out too much, the cigarettes would burn it back to an agreeable length.

How the hell was I going to deliver pizzas in that car?

"What up, Big Dave!"

Maniacal Mikey Bishop had stepped out of his

neighboring house trailer on his way to his lucrative job sell-ing funny books to socially inept virgins at the local comic book shop. He was already three bong hits into his day and sucking fanatically at his vape.

I narrowed my eyes at the sumbitch. Could he be responsible? Was he secretly my archnemesis? The horned trickster to my flying viking?

"Hey, man, you got a big cock painted on your Chevy."

"Your powers of observation like your beard are tru-ly otherworldly. Erk. Erk. Maybe you'll get that spot on the X-Mens, yet."

"Don't be a dick, Big Dave. And would it kill you to bring back a pizza to share?"

"Yeah, it might. I wish you well."

I watched him hop into his dickless Subaru and fuck off toward the comic shop.

The more I thought about it, the less likely Maniacal Mikey Bishop seemed the supervillain sort. Also, it took me five minutes to hop online and see that he was livestreaming on his YouTube Channel, hooting and hollering about some horseshit Marvel movie with ray guns and samurai swords and superpowers for the entire duration of my Mister Joe's sojourn last night. Still, while he may not have painted the cock, I had a feeling he approved of it.

Fuck, I hated playing detective in a world where ev-eryone was a suspect.

In the shadow of Chicago, I put on my Pittsburgh Steelers coat, the last defense against the polar wind channeling down Lake Michigan from the artic regions of Northern Canada. Of course, the jacket made me a target for every self-respecting, mustachioed, Bears' fan living within a fifty-mile radius of my house trailer and the five taverns I frequented. Any one of whom could have painted a giant dick on my Aveo.

I drove out to Gussie's Pizzeria to start my shift. The Aveo drew more attention than I was used to. I nodded my head and snap finger pointed at the passing motorists who felt the need to acknowledge the giant dick on the car.

I parked around back; thankful Gussie hadn't yet roused himself from last night's drunk.

Shannon had green hair today. Every puncture wound was adorned with pieces of colorful costume jewelry. Felix the pizza cook was still Mexican. His mustache still resembled hash marks penciled in by an indifferent god. There wasn't much the poor bastard could do with himself.

Shannon said "hey Big Dave, I noticed on your way in you got a big cock painted on your car."

"It's not that big."

"It covers your entire car."

"It's a small car."

"Whatever."

"Did you do it?" I asked.

"What? Paint that dick? No way. Why would I paint a cock on your car?"

There were plenty of reasons. Chief among them, my bowel movement misadventures in the bathrooms of her duplex. I didn't care to bring that up in conversation. Her shocked response seemed authentic enough to scratch her name off my shit list. I knew without a doubt Felix was innocent. The cock lacked the artistic flair Mexican graffiti was famous for.

"I'm just asking everybody is all," I said. "I'm trying to be as diligent with this cock investigation as my nerves allow. Just do me a favor and don't tell Gussie about that cock on my car."

"Are you delivering pizzas like that?"

"Can I borrow your Celica?"

"No."

"Then, I'm delivering pizza like this."

"Just don't let Gussie see it. He won't be happy."

"Gussie's probably the prick that did it. While he was in one of his alcoholic fugues."

Gussie was my neighbor on Sheffield Avenue for the entirety of my childhood. He put me to work when no one else was interested in employing a big guy with zero skills, an assload of social anxiety and the occasional nervous tic. Gussie opened Gussie's Pizzeria around the time I began drinking legally, and I've been mostly the sole delivery driver ever since. You might question what a Dutch/Polack like Gussie knows about making pizzas. I got the answer. He bought the recipe off that fucking Greek, Larry the Pizza Man when he retired. It's a phenomenal pizza, everything baked under the cheese with a quarter ounce of herbs and spices sprinkled throughout.

Too much information? That's just my way of mentioning that I'm a small part of the history of The Region's pizza pie legacy. I was there when Larry the Pizza Man passed the pizza man mantle on to Gussie the Spastic. I have value. I don't deserve a big dick painted on my Aveo.

Gussie also owned about two dozen rental houses. He was The Region's answer to Donald Trump complete with a mail order bride, though his was Guatemalan. Gussie adored purchasing borderline condemned houses from the poors who could not afford the necessary renovations to make their homes livable again. He'd give them pennies on the dollar and provide them with references for the section eight apartments on the blighted south side of town. Gussie also kept an army of crack addicts on his payroll. Pederasts, addicts, degenerates. If you were a deviant and could swing a hammer straight, Gussie put you to work renovating houses you might have smoked crack within the week before. Everyone got paid in dope and fed pizzas I'd have to deliver with no expectation of a tip.

I mention this because any one of those free-basing cocksuckers could have painted that dick on my Aveo. Every one of those assholes were jealous of me because I had cash money in my pocket, a fairly new though embarrassing car, the love and respect of my family, and for a brief and glorious time, an exceptional winter jacket. Was this reason enough for a confederacy of perverts to deface my car? Who knows what kind of aberrant thoughts fizzle through the dope vaporized minds of these janky sons-a-bitches.

When I expressed my theories to Shannon, she reacted with a suspicious amount of skepticism.

"That dick didn't paint itself," I reasoned.

"I'm sure there's a reason," she said. "I just don't think that's the one."

I was primed to argue more but she reminded me of my duties, delivering Greek by way of Dutch/Polish style pizzas and calzones to the hungry men doing God's work at the BP refinery. I attached the Gussie's Pizzeria delivery sign to the right testicle atop the Aveo and got to work.

If anyone noticed the giant cock painted across the car during my deliveries, they were kind enough not to ridicule me. I studied their faces, however, looking for a flicker of recognition, a flash of expression of the sort that would implicate them as the artist confronted by their handiwork in the wild. The culprit could have easily been a dissatisfied customer expressing their disappointment with a crudely drawn cock on my car rather than a strongly worded one-star Yelp review. Nothing.

I went to bed that night having drank the better part of a case of Michelob no closer to solving the enigma of the genital-befouled Aveo as I was the moment I stepped out of Mister Joe's Tavern.

In the morning, lying on my too-small bed, tangled up in sheets, my mind did not have to venture far to find a god-awful memory to torture myself with. In this moment, I replayed the Mohawk's Reception Incident over and over in my mind.

This was back when I was doing most of my serious drinking at the Stumble Inn on Burnham Avenue. This had to be every bit of twelve years ago. I was underaged, but it helped that since the age of fourteen I've looked like a forty-year-old man. Back then, I was a hundred pounds lighter and still harbored hope I could become a medical transcriptionist at one of the hospital megaplexes that had been cropping up on the city fringes ever since it was discovered that every fucking thing in The Region caused cancer.

At the Stumble Inn, Ralph Pawlecki and Julie Vargo were the celebrity couple du jour. Ralph made his living pounding beers and announcing to anyone in his orbit that he was a skilled bricklayer momentarily in between jobs. Julie earned her money working as a paralegal for her father. Apparently, he doted on his daughter and gave her everything she wanted which I assumed were mostly Little Debbie snack cakes on account of her gargantuan size.

That's not to pass judgement, mind you. I understand in this day and age we are to extend every bit of grace and understanding we can to people who are not six foot tall, two hundred pound, well-muscled, white males between the ages of twenty and thirty-eight with their hair just right, and their cocks where it needs to be, educated, but not too well-read, Christian, but not necessarily practicing, and financially secure enough to ward off any catastrophes should the lucky stars misalign.

So, Julie, like myself, was due some grace and understanding, but, sadly, there's none to be had here for any of us. She was every bit of three hundred pounds, but not in a sexy way. Her flesh hung off her bones in such a fashion, one would naturally assume she recently weighed three-fifty but rapidly lost the fifty pounds due to a sudden, diarrhetic illness. Which is to say, I took my shot at Julie when I first met her, and she shut me down, cold. Ralph must have been a charming motherfucker, sober. I'd never known him to be sober.

When they decided to get married, everyone who'd had the misfortune of having to watch them play kissy face at the bar were invited to the wedding and the following reception at the Mohawk's Club. Whether I approved of the nuptials or not, it was an open bar.

A free dead nazi was not to be had, however. The promise of an open bar was so loud, I missed the rumors of choice limitations. The server acted as though she'd never heard of Rumplemintz before. I settled for rum and cokes. It must have done the job, though. When it was time for the groom to peel the garter off the bride's thigh, I found myself loitering around the dance floor with the other single, drunken schlubs.

And we were all single for a reason. A skinful of booze did little to ease my social anxiety. I was surrounded mostly by strangers. I knew my tic was in full effect. I was "erk…erking" all over the place, and I was still the most de-sirable, eligible bachelor in that entire fucking hall.

We all tried to avoid gazing at the dead white ex-panse of Julie's thigh as Ralph yanked at the elastic fabric. He didn't give us much chance to prepare before he slung the garter over his shoulder so quickly I scarcely realized the garter had looped around my forearm until I went to take a gulp of my rum and coke.

While the bouquet was tossed, I sat at the Stumble Inn table near the back of the reception hall and studied the hula hoop of lace and silk dangling from my hand. I glanced at the drunken Polack seated next to me. His googly eyes peered somewhere over my right shoulder.

"Look at this," I said. "I bet I could fit this thing around my fucking waist."

The Polack gurgled some kind of response. I took it as a challenge, so I bent down, pressed my legs together, and worked the garter over my shoes and up my legs. It got a little tight around my hips, but I persevered. The garter fit around my waist just fine. To be fair to Julie, though, I'd yet to put on my winter weight.

I didn't think about the garter again until the deejay requested the lady who caught the bouquet and the gen-tleman who caught the garter please come to the stage for pictures.

Now, you can blame the booze, you might even hint I'm an idiot, but I swear I failed to realize that fucking garter was still around my waist until I hit the stage. The horrified gasps clued me in. All around me loomed a conspiracy of indignant bordering on furious faces. You'd have thought I was the sorriest bastard alive the way they treated me.

Any one of those people could have painted that cock on my Aveo. Not Ralph and Julie, though. They got killed in a fiery automobile accident five years ago. Don't drink and drive, kids.

So, that was the nightmare scenario that got me out of bed. I'd made up my mind to grab groceries this morning after smoking my breakfast cigarette and indulging in a few leftover beers.

I like to do my shopping in the morning since I mostly hate interacting with people if I can help it, and mornings in The Region offers a scarcity of citizens due to the rampant alcoholism that keeps the population behind closed doors nursing hangovers as the sun crawls across broken glass toward its zenith.

There's always an exception to the rule, though. Despite the gathering storm clouds, I parked my car at the very back of the lot so as not to offend the Parkview shopper's delicate sensibilities. My humanity in the face of painted cocks gifted me a half mile trek to the sliding doors. I muttered curses the entire walk. I'm not built for fucking marathons; I just didn't want to deal with any hard looks or difficult questions I might have put to me. The exception to the rule in this case was personified by an old black guy standing out front as if he'd been waiting for me all morning.

"Hey, yo, dawg."

"Yes… dawg?"

"Let me axe you a question."

Fuck. "No, I don't know who painted a giant dick on my car, though, I actually do believe the black community is not responsible for this one. It feels very much like a white-on-white crime."

"What? Naw, man. Shit. Man wants a painted cock on his car, what business is it of mine? Naw, I just gotta axe you why you wearing a Steelers coat the day before you know them Bears and the damn Packers gots a game?"

I considered this question, standing outside the Parkview Grocery Store, a store which, incidentally, gave no view of any parks, whatsoever. There was not a park within a ten-mile radius of the store. Parks, here, were scarce since there were more pedophiles per capita in The Region than anywhere else in the country if you discount the entirety of the south. I considered the skinny, old black man who posed this question. He might not have been out here pan-handling, but he was definitely loitering. Why? He seemed seriously distressed by the jacket fate had forced me to wear. All I wanted was a Stoufer's Gramma's Rice Bake, a two liter of Faygo Red Pop, maybe some Vitner's Barbecue flavored potato chips and fifty dollars' worth of whatever else jumped out at me. That's all I wanted out of this shitty life.

I didn't want to have to field these sorts of existential questions. Not with a big dick painted on my car.

Why was I wearing a coat emblazoned with the emblems of a football team I held in contempt while driving a car I absolutely despised, adorned with a big dick I did not approve of?

How did I become a victim of my own life? My choices never rightfully felt like my choices. Why?

"Let me ask you this," I said. "What has a bear ever done for you, my man? Besides, I guess, tearing the hell out of white people stupid enough to go hiking out in the middle of nowhere. But steel workers… Steel workers built this country. Now, you may not like this country. I sure fucking don't. But we can both agree it was built. And we got the steel workers we can thank for that."

"What the hell's that got to do with football?"

"Exactly."

I gave him the double finger snapping finger point, wished him well, and continued into the store with its fairly tame sampling of societal horrors and utterly egregious examples of Capitalism run amok. While gathering all the snacks I needed for survival, the clouds opened and released a deluge of rain. I listened to the torrent hammering the roof as I wondered how a small bag of Teriyaki flavored beef jerky could cost twelve dollars. I'd hoped to beat the storm this morning, but those extra post sunrise beers proved my undoing. By making an innocent choice, I'd fucked myself, again.

The black guy had mercifully abandoned his post

by the time I exited Parkview. The rain showed no signs of abating. I trudged the length of the parking lot carrying my soaked groceries. Rain pissed down on me.

I stood there for a long moment almost failing to recognize my Aveo. The down pour had washed away the cock leaving behind a perfectly unremarkable vehicle. I blinked my eyes against the rain. This was also some sort of judgement against me, I decided. By refraining from slapping the black guy for asking jackassy questions, I'd proven to the gods I didn't deserve a big dick painted on my car. That had to be it. I still felt deeply ashamed of the car, though.

Piper of the Hipsters

He called himself Piper. I hated Piper immediately. Not that I'm the sort of guy given to fits of irrational prejudice. I have called for the extermination of the Amish in the past, but it never went beyond idle threats and internet propaganda, a couple harsh tweets. Nothing that alarmed the Mennonites in the Tennessee Valley.

My hatred for Piper, though, that was legitimate. The way he wore his long hair twisted up and settled on top of his head, his lumberjack beard, the Grecian style sandals, all of this only confirmed my suspicions this man was a member of the hipster tribe.

He called himself Piper, but it was I who named him Suckadickocles.

When he entered Whole Foods for his job interview, Joe and I, entrenched in the meat department, marked his arrival the moment he dismounted his fixed gear bicycle.

"This man is prettier than I am," I muttered, sensing the approaching social upheaval sure to unseat me as alpha sexy papa wolf among the middle-aged ladies scarfing down tiramisus in the bakery.

Joe didn't answer, trapped as he was in his own display case of chicken-slinging misery. At the moment, he was tied up with a woman well into her sixties who demanded a length of Alabama sausage and would not take a confused grimace for an answer.

Whole Foods carried a wide, wild and varied selection of sausage. Chorizo, apple chicken, Polish, Italian. Irish bangers for those who preferred the wee sausages. Nothing in the way of an Alabama sausage. It simply did not exist.

"It's this big," the lady explained, holding her hands a foot apart. "And this big around," making a very unrealistic circle with her veiny hands.

"Nope," Joe sighed. "Help me out here, buddy."

I assured the lady while we did not come equipped with sausages of that magnitude, Joe had certainly seen a few Alabama sausages up close and personal in his day.

"I can't tell if she was fucking with me or not," Joe said as the lady disappointedly nudged her cart toward the morons in the deli.

Joe was a career meat man, thirty-five years slinging chickens, slicing steaks, grinding clods into chuck. I was three months into my tour. Very early into my employment we found we shared a common coping mechanism. Sailor Jerry's spiced Caribbean rum.

By the time Joe and I ducked back into the freezer for a couple salutes to the commanding officer and returned to action, Piper had become Whole Foods' newest deli employee.

"Why on earth hire a goofy sumbitch looks like a love child of Mifune and one of those Duck Dynasty jackasses?"

"To keep the gals coming back for more macaroni," Joe said. Thirty-five years. He had seen it all before.

Then it was Tuesday before I knew it. The one day of the week the Whole Foods masterminds lowered the price of chicken breast and ground chuck to the diabolically scant price of $2.99 a pound. So, it was all hands on deck in the meat department. Of course, the rest of the six-man crew saw fit to disappear when Gramma Satan appeared at the counter. Her glittery blue eyes affixed me as though she were a poultry-lusting ancient mariner and I, the luckless wedding guest.

She got right to it. "Thirteen pounds of ground beef. And you can bag them by the half pound."

"Goddam, dirty carnivorous bitch. I'm gonna punch you right in the flabby neck," I muttered, Popeye-style, so she couldn't quite make out the words.

Bagging twenty-six half pound balls of ground beef is the Bataan death march of the meat-slinging business. There's nothing good about it, seems like it takes forever, and, at the end of it, you don't feel any real grand sense of accomplishment.

In a whirl of flying ground beef, I glanced up and saw Piper leisurely scooping potato salad into a plastic cup for an adoring mother of three. Fuck, if I had a corncob pipe, I'd fill it with canned spinach and whip his hipster ass to such a devastating degree he'd need every last one of Mumford's sons to help him into his plaid rompers and tuck him into bed for a troubled night plagued with dreams reliving the vicious head-stomping I delivered.

"God bless you," Gramma Satan smiled serenely as she toddled away with her basket brimming with ground chuck.

"I hope God strikes you down with the pox."

Just then the other five meat, chicken and seafood men materialized around me, every last one of them smelling pleasantly of spiced rum. Jay, the meat manager, showed his remorse at abandoning me in my darkest fifteen minutes by offering me a smoke break.

Smoke breaks were so important to me, I'd actually taken up smoking to fully appreciate them. I was now the only employee who smoked cigarettes in the meat department. Everyone else sucked vapors from odd, mechanical, cock-like instruments. This is just me talking, but I'm of the opinion, anyone who will suck on a vape will suck an android's dick.

Coming around the corner into the common area, I saw Piper laconically leaned against a desk studying his fingernails in a posture some fools would describe as the epitome of cool.

The Gramma Satan incident had my blood up; all I could think about was how badly I wanted to karate chop this man in the face space between his manbun and pointy chin beard.

Still, making fleeting eye contact, I felt the impulse to acknowledge his existence. "How are you?"

In seemingly slow motion, he treated me to the

slightest uplift of the chin. His eyes hooded perhaps God's spotlight shining down upon him. "S'up," he lisped.

My mind recoiled in horror, leaving me speechless and vaguely dazed. I stumbled away, muttering, much in the same way my grandfather travelled in his later years.

I wanted to say "When I talk to you, talk to me like a man, not a Backstreet Boy." But my chance for witty retorts had dissolved. I tried to trivialize the encounter; that it was just a goofy hipster sending out a childish greeting to his cultural superior, and I mostly believed this. Yet why did I continually call for his torture and execution while shadow-boxing bags of organic potato chips?

The chin diss incident as the brief encounter came to be known swelled out of all reasonable proportion. Mostly because I repeated the story at least a hundred times a day for a week, often to complete strangers. Even Gramma Satan seemed perplexed by my irrational hatred for hipsters. Her crystal blue eyes shined with a malicious dementia as I described the slow uplift of his needlessly bearded chin, the slitted eyes, the drawn out "s'up."

"Should I have just judo chopped him? Should I have gone full on Pei Mei and just obliterated the entire Tennessee Valley clan of hipsters? Rousting them from their artist colonies, massacring them at their microbrew tasting parties, inconveniencing them at their coffee klatch poetry readings?"

"Seventeen pounds of ground chuck. Can I have those in ten one-pound bags, ten half-pound bags, and eight quarter-pound bags. I'm shopping for some friends at church."

"No," I decided. "No, you and your church friends cannot have your meat separated in that bullshit manner. Can I come around the counter and throttle your throat until Satan himself rises from the depths of hell to harvest your rotten soul?"

And that's how I lost my job at Whole Foods. On my way out the door, I flashed Suckadickocles the middle finger. My anger appeared to confuse him. He raised what I thought to be a completely unwarranted peace sign. And that, I figured, ended my involvement with Piper of the hipsters. That was that.

But that was not that!

At 1:20 in the am central standard time, I was called to the Circle K to meet my cocaine connection, but my cocaine connection did not show.

Upon exiting my minivan, I was immediately accosted and aggressively jostled by three men. Hipsters, judging by their corduroy shorts, sculpted beards, horned-rimmed glasses and interestingly pointless tattoos.

I could smell espresso on the breath of the leader as he whispered, "Piper sends his regards."

At one point I was kicked repeatedly in the face by what can only be described as a red Converse. Despite my Pei Mei remark to Gramma Satan, I never wanted my all-consuming prejudice against hipster douchebags to turn violent.

But it had. It had. And, in a surprising turn of events, I was the victim.

The police were no help. They are not equipped to seek out three men riding fixed gear bicycles, one who sings show tunes while striking me upside the head with a rolled up, vintage poster of Jodorowsky's "Holy Mountain." You would think skinny jeans hampers the kung fu. It does not.

As it stands, now, I'm attempting to recover from the severe wounds to my psyche, to say nothing of the bruising around my right calf and left shoulder. Unironic prayers are needed.

Snowballs in Hell

We lived on the ass end of Lake Michigan, just outside Chicago. When the chimney effect channeled artic cold from Canada down the length of the lake, all that ice and snow, the frigidity and misery, it all landed right on top of our heads. And we loved it. Of course, by we, I mean me and my crew, and we ranged in age from eleven to thirteen. So, we couldn't tote a thimbleful of good sense between the lot of us.

Back then, around January in The Region, we'd race the darkness and ensuing blizzards home from school.

I'd dump my nearly empty bookbag in the corner of my closet-sized room and race to put on as many layers of clothes as possible. I usually succeeded in layering five sweatpants and five sweatshirts. Only a poverty of wardrobe disallowed six layers. A woolen Bogan for my head, stupid moon boots for my feet, a good pair of thermal gloves that allowed for finger dexterity, and a quick acknowledgement to my mother, and I'd charge out the door into the streets, searching for my partners in mischief.

In the light of the streetlamps, the snowflakes swirled like a cadre of starlings synchronized in their patterns of flight. The winter bare trees fractured into the vividly dark blue sky creating black rifts in the fabric of reality that a twelve-year-old could leap through into a more adventurous dimension if he took a mind to. That's what it looked like to me, anyway, and I understood inherently I needed to keep these kinds of observations to myself. The other fellas would think I was weird, maybe borderline gay.

Months earlier, during a trip to the bookstore, I happened upon a paperback with an eye-catching cover that appealed to my horror-loving aesthetic. I'd never heard of the author, Clive Barker, before. According to the cover blurb, Stephen King seemed to think he was a big deal, and that was good enough for me. Since reading "In the Flesh," I felt as though my eyes had grown more attuned to the magic in the ordinary, the poetry in the mundane.

Tonight, with the new snow thickening on the ground and obliterating the streets, I was looking not so much for poetry as trouble. The fallen snow was the perfect dampness for packing. Every five feet I trudged, I scooped a snowball and launched it at stop signs, street signs, and the picture windows of the nearest houses.

On the corner of Hohman Avenue and 142nd, I met up with Vic Koselke, the youngest of the Koselke brothers, and the youngest of our gang of miscreants. His oldest brother worked as a clean-up boy at the Northside Bakery and was already fermenting his own strawberry wine which made him a neighborhood legend. The middle brother, William, was my age but didn't care to run the streets amid a blizzard, opting instead to stay locked inside playing video games. Vic was always down for mischief. He was the most accomplished thief I knew in a group of kids who all prided themselves on their abilities to steal. Half the Iron Maiden and all the Quiet Riot cassettes in my collection were stolen by Vic from the Zayre department store. I was trying unsuccessfully to convince him to try his hand at stealing paperback books, but he remained disinterested no matter how much I tried to convince him that reading was the cornerstone of culture.

Vic wore a top layer of camouflage that seemed ridiculous to me given the white out conditions. Maybe I was just envious. My own father refused to provide me with adequate camouflage, correctly surmising I was neither a hunter nor a soldier.

Vic and I threw snowballs at each other until we closed the distance enough to become accurate. We continued packing the snow in our hands, eyeballing one another, hesitant to make the first move. Our Mexican stand-off was interrupted by an actual Mexican, Armando Blanco, who with his layers of clothing was as big around as he was tall. Symanski followed close behind. Four was a good number to start the troublemaking we decided.

During the preceding years when the blizzards would hit, we got a kick out of skeeching off the back of car bumpers. The old folks driving these cars lacked the sense to remain inside in these conditions. A whiteout blizzard with zero visibility and a negative eight-degree windchill, and these old Polish ladies refused to stand down from converging on Saint Casimir Church to recite their novenas.

We'd loiter at the stop sign beneath the shadow of the church steeple. With anybody stupid enough to obey the traffic laws, we'd creep behind their cars and latch on to their back bumpers.

Some nights, there'd be four or five of us hanging off the back bumper of Gramma's Buick, our bodies slipping and sliding along the snowy streets, as the clueless driver navigated the snowy roads. Each one of us likely imagined we were Indiana Jones hanging from the back of a Nazi truck. We'd fight to knock each other off the moving vehicle. Sometimes, we would succeed in grabbing hold of the ankles of a kid gripping a back bumper, another kid would grab his ankles, and you'd find yourself part of a human chain like the monkeys in a barrel game, hooked to the back of a Oldsmobile.

That all stopped when a dude delivering pies for Gussie's Pizzeria stopped and pulled a gun out on us. It was an oddly antiquated gun with what looked like a flint lock, but I didn't stop to study his firearm too closely, mortified with fear as I was. Apparently, we were beginning to age out of those type of shenanigans, looking like grown ass men as we ran up on these vehicles, and it was starting to make these hapless drivers act a little squirrelly.

We began the night tossing snowballs at the younger kids who were just trying to get in some sledding down the overpass embankment. When that got old, we agreed to trudge toward Olympia Lanes figuring we could rain down snowball hell on the dedicated bowlers moving between their cars and the bowling alley.

Halfway there, we stopped at Egghead's house and got him to come out and join us. We called John "Egghead" for reasons that escaped me. He wasn't particularly smart by any metric we measured ourselves against. His head was no more egg-shaped than any other head I'd encountered. He disliked the nickname which gave us all the reason we needed to solidify his moniker into our conversational routine. Hell, they called me "Corndigger," and that name didn't make a lick of sense to me, either.

Egghead wore Denver Broncos attire which baffled us since we were neck deep in Chicago Bears country, this being back in the mid-eighties when they fielded an exceptional team, and, as far as I knew, Egghead had never ventured west of Joliet, Illinois.

Egghead stepped off his porch and immediately packed a snowball. We followed suit. As we reached the street, a pine green Chevy Cordoba eased down the road. The snow was six inches deep on the street. With parked cars lining either side of the road, there was little margin for error for the driver of the land yacht. I figured by the time he reached the corner; we'd launch a fusillade of snowballs on the poor bastard.

Egghead had other ideas. He walked to within three feet of the passing car and blasted it right in the driver's side window. The tightly packed snowball sounded like a cannonball thudding against glass.

We froze for one delicious moment. The air was so cold and crisp it felt as though you could bite into the air, and it would crack like the scrim of ice atop a glass of water left out in the frigid weather. Everything was snow and silence as we considered how urgently we needed to run away.

The Cordoba coasted another ten feet then stopped.

The door sprung open, and I was off like a jackrabbit. I didn't even see the interior light illuminate the driver. I rushed through Egghead's backyard, launching myself over Chainlink fences as quickly as my five layers of clothing allowed. I was aware of the rest of the fellas sprinting in different directions.

I hopped another fence which took me into the alley. Here, I hesitated. I looked to my right. Vic sprinted toward the end of the alley. The camouflage wasn't doing a damn thing to obscure his escape. I anticipated the Cordoba would drive around enter the alley from that direction. I thought better than to call after Vic. The dumbass would have to learn the hard way.

Symanski and Blanco hopped the fence directly in front of us and continued racing through yards which was a safe and logical path. I was just tired of scaling fences. I just wasn't built for these extended escape scenarios. My inherent laziness would not allow for prolonged adventure.

To my left, I saw Egghead trundling down the alley, and this seemed to be the most viable path of least resistance. I jogged after him, enjoying the sensation of the cold air entering my lungs and exploding from my mouth in foggy plumes.

Egghead cut left into a yard half a block down. I reached this point quickly and found there was only a knee length of plywood to circumvent. Egghead had quit running. He stood a scant ten feet ahead of me. His back was toward me. He had his hands on his head to control his breathing as we'd been taught in basketball practice.

As I stepped over the plywood, I became instantly aware of what sounded like batwings flapping, along with a freakish gasping for breath. I looked up, and the driver was almost upon me, having followed the length of the alley.

The dumb bastard wasn't dressed for this weather. He wore a pair of jeans that were already soaked through to the knees. He wore a band T-shirt advertising some group "Five Guys Named Schmoe" which sounded like some kind of hipster shit to me. He wore an unzipped motorcycle jacket over this, the leather flapping maniacally as he charged like a wild-eyed locomotive.

I made a choice here. I chose my own well-being at the expense of Egghead's welfare. I ran past Egghead like a ninja. Now, I've watched ninja movies my entire youth. This was the one time I successfully moved like a ninja. I ran past Egghead deadly quiet without a word of warning.

You always hear the old joke about the bear attack. The one that goes, I don't have to run faster than the bear, I just have to run faster than you. Well, I've put this in action, and let me tell you, it's every bit as satisfying as you'd think it would be.

Egghead didn't know what hit him. At first, anyway. I imagined he got clued in pretty fucking quick by the third or fourth punch. The driver pounced on Egghead, knocking him into the snow as if he were preparing to make snow angels. He immediately began to ground and pound the kid.

"You think this shit's funny, you little motherfucker."

Fists rained down on John's not entirely egg-like head.

"You fucking kids think it's cool to shit on me? Jesus Christ. Every time I turn around, I got somebody fucking with me."

Egghead was taking his beating silently. It's how I preferred to suffer through my beatings as well, though I didn't always succeed in this.

My first thought was this goofy bastard's going to kill John. My second thought: I better get the fuck out of here before I'm next.

I continued running through the yard, across the driveway which led me right back to the street where this all began.

The Cordoba remained parked in the middle of the road, half a block away. The driver's side door was opened. The interior light continued to shine. Exhaust puffed from the tailpipe.

I jogged toward the car, though every fiber of common sense my Polish Heritage imbued me with warned against it. As I neared the car, Vic stepped out of the shadows of an elm tree as if stepping from an extradimensional rift torn through the fabric of reality.

"Holy shit," Vic said. "You see where that guy went?"

I hooked a thumb over my shoulder. "He's back there giving Egghead the business."

Vic shrugged. "Serves him right, I suppose."

"Yeah, fuck him."

Vic smiled dangerously. I recognized that smile. It was the smile of an eleven-year-old about to talk a thirteen-year-old into doing something incredibly stupid.

"You wanna go for a ride?" He asked.

"In that piece of shit Chevy?"

"Sure. Why not. He's got it coming."

"We could get in some serious trouble."

"From who? Nobody knows who we are. Blanco and Symanski are probably home by now sipping on hot chocolate. What's Egghead gonna say? This dude just beat the shit out of a twelve-year-old, how quick is he going to the cops with that?"

I felt myself wavering. I sensed I was on the verge of doing something bad on a life-altering scale.

"Hell, yeah," Vic continued. "We'll just drive this bad boy down the block. Maybe drive it out toward Lincoln school. Park it out of the way and skeech our way back home."

"I got a better idea."

I reached into the car and turned off the ignition. I withdrew the car keys and held the ring up to the illumination of the streetlight. There were ten, twelve keys on the ring, likely house keys, work keys, garage keys. I balled them in my gloved fist and threw them as hard as I could into a snowbank across the street.

"Corndigger, you're a bad man."

"Almost the worst," I agreed. "Now let's get the fuck out of here. Hopefully, Egghead ain't been killed."

We ducked into the shadows and made our way back to the house while the snowplows and salt trucks went to work.

I'd just made a man's bad day infinitely worse. And I kept my good day from becoming the sort of hell I'd find no escape from.

Ninjas, Hipsters and Nazis

Anyone who claims to know me understands there are three things I legitimately hate in this life. During any given day, I'm confronted with an untold number of targets requiring the focus of my animosity but for the sake of this piece, I'm going to concentrate on the three hatreds which have consumed me the entirety of my life.

Ninjas. Hipsters. Nazis.

My early life, haunting arcade halls and video game palaces, retiring home to an 8-bit Nintendo existence, conditioned me to believe one day in the not-so-distant future, I would find myself casually strolling along the top of an eighteen-wheeler (parked, of course, I'm not going to strain credulity by even suggesting the possibility of loitering atop a moving semi-truck), minding my own business when, leaping out from the edges of reality, a barrage of lily white gangbangers wearing denim and swatches of fabric concealing their identities would attack for no good reason, flinging Chinese stars before charging with katana swords raised precariously above their heads.

My entire youth I wore sleeveless muscle shirts in preparation for just such an event. If I learned anything from studying Michael Dudikoff films on late night HBO, it's that, as formidable as ninjas are, they can be handily defeated with a continuous barrage of front punches and roundhouse kicks. Even though I can count on one balled fist the amount of ninja confrontations I've been subjected to I still despise turtles to this day. And certain food processors.

Hipsters are a much more insidious and prevalent enemy. Your average hipster will favor a samurai more than a ninja, what with their silly top knots and odd code of behavior and a smug love for Kurosawa films which they will work into any conversation lasting longer than two minutes.

Use to be, I waged open warfare on the Amish. My intense annoyance with those peanut brittle slinging, electricity adverse rope smokers was such that I couldn't strut past a horse drawn carriage without keying the sides or hobbling a hoof. Now, I know it's chickenshit to assault a man's ride. Ordinarily, I don't go mucking about with a hipster's Tesla or a Nazi's Dodge Charger or a ninja's… Ninja, but the Amish exist outside the man code of conduct for urban conflict. I posit that if you purposefully chose to live beyond the realm of modern society then the usual rules cease to apply.

It's a moot point, anyway. I single-handedly canceled Rumspringa for those water-pumping assholes a long time ago, knocking them all the way back to their little gas-lit communities in Tennessee, and, perhaps, Pennsylvania, where such aberrant behavior as baking bread and smushing strawberries into jam is tolerated.

Wonder why you don't see the Amish haunting the aisles of Alabama Wal-marts like Poltergeist sequel villains? It is because I bested them. With some Polish good sense and a few stalwarts of twenty-first century technology, I dismantled some two hundred years of their civilization's progression. But that is a story for another day.

So now I've replaced the Amish with the Hipster. The names have changed only the beards remain the same. Rest assured, in keeping with my personal zero tolerance policy, if I hear Mumford and Sons, I take out the man listening to it, usually while he tries to lecture me on the superior sound quality of vinyl. I see a pair of skinny jeans; I karate chop the chap wearing them usually while he indulges an orange peel scented microbrew and subtly puffs a corn-cob pipe between pulls off his raspberry and dragon fruit infused vape contraption.

I believe I hate the Hipster most of all, and I know at the very least, they seek to discredit my continued boasts of personal genius, if not outright undermine my superior grooviness.

Attempts to communicate with the Hipster are futile. Here I am, seeking to sing the praise of the latest entry in the Marvel Cinematic Universe and the Hipster interrupts me with a diatribe on the ethereal beauty of Jim Harrison's poetry. Let me tell you something, mister, I've read *After Ikkyu and Other Poems* and I'm not impressed with Harrison's wordsmithing. But *Doctor Strange* is awesome, thank you very much.

The Hipster will accuse you of cultural appropriation when you don a Cher wig and eagle feather draped deer skins before hitting up the annual Three Floyd Halloween Bacchanalia where you drink copious amounts of firewater and bemoan the white man's iron horse that has forever altered your land and lifestyle unless the government mollifies you with either a bullet or a casino, yet the Hipster will deny any appropriations of their own, despite the Jesus sandals, the man buns, and the ridiculously dense beards that warn the populace these Hipsters are merely one banjo solo away from anally raping the next unfortunate out-of-towner. To say nothing of the cultural appropriation of full-body tattoos. Back in the day, if you were covered in tattoos, especially of the facial variety, it meant that you were a mean motor scooter. Now, any asshole who can recite thirty-five styles of latte can get a skinful of ink.

The battle between myself and the Hipster has grown fierce as of late. Just last week, the Scurrilous Six (once known as the Vituperative Five), a well-known yet comfortably obscure gang of hipster scalliwags, initiated a drive-by on my home, pedaling past on their fixed gear bicycles, firing off antique blunderbusses which left a slew of silverware and calligraphy pens embedded in my vinyl siding for three days. Of course, this was in retaliation for the time I firebombed the local organic produce stand, destroying a month's supply of locally harvested honey and several stalks of celery.

The morning before this, the Hipster accosted my son near the chessboard at an eastside coffeehouse because he was my son and had the audacity to order a simple black coffee. The Hipster assaulted my son with such verbal vitriol and physical ferocity, my boy was left shaken, with discomfort in his left wrist from a culturally misappropriated Indian burn and a fleeting bout of lightheadedness brought on by all the hazelnut/butternut squash scented vape fumes my son inhaled during the altercation.

I'm weighing my next move very carefully.

Which brings me to last and, perhaps, the most ridiculous entry on my abbreviated list of vehement repugnance, the Hipster's kissing cousin, the modern-day American Nazi, indistinguishable from the Hipster in terms of beard cultivation and the appreciation of a good pair of suspenders to hold the britches up, a throwback to their shared ancestral fashionistas, the Amish.

Man, just the term American Nazi makes as much sense as the moniker Polish scientist. The mind rebels against the paradoxical implications.

Concerning my hatred for these silly bastards, it's not that I condemn their rampart racism. I, too, have dabbled in a little tribalism in my time, specifically against the Lithuanians, two of whom are my downstairs neighbors, both disagreeable men burdened with odd practices from the old country, like the habit of pounding the ceiling with broomsticks when their joy runs cold.

The Hipster I can understand, even respect how diligently they adhere to their misbegotten beliefs, such as how a Hipster will continue to vehemently profess a preference for European cinema over American movies, even under the torturous duress of watching a Jared Leto movie. The Nazi will cry their hatred of the black man to heavens, unless a black man happens to be in the immediate vicinity. When confronted with the living embodiment of their doctrine of hate, the modern Nazi will become surprisingly amicable and compliant, going so far as to offer up the sexual favors of their own sweet mothers in order to keep the peace.

Unpredictable rivers of racism run from the goofy font of modern day Americanized Nazism. Why the hatred of Jews? Most of these jackasses wouldn't know a Jew if he crawled up the Nazi's Aryan leg and bit him on the matzoh balls. And what, exactly, is the Nazi afraid the Jew is going to replace him at? Sister fucking?

Here's a history lesson for the uninformed. American Nazism as we know it today is, actually and factually, an offshoot of the Howdy Doody fan club which militarized back in '58 in the hopes of protecting members from the anal ravaging visited upon them by African Americans run amok. This also explains the Nazi's partiality for suspenders clipped to their britches.

I stomp Nazis as a matter of course. And they know it. You've never seen a tiki torch extinguished so quickly as when I come on the scene. Chants of "blood and soil" turn to "love one, love all" when I appear in their midst. I will introduce their blood to soil so fast it will make their swastika tattoos spin like windmills.

So, these are the three things in life I hate. Ninjas, Hipsters, and Nazis. Actually, make it four. I'm still not done with the Amish, yet, looking so smug with their rampant pubic hair and manual plows.

Some folks will have you believe it's not right to hate anyone. These gandhis are no better than the Nazis in their inability to see the world through my eyes. They've never been given the stink eye by some Amish peanut-sheller because I parked my horseless carriage in amidst their pumpkin patches.

They've never gone to Wal-mart to buy some tiki

torches to keep mosquitos at bay from a Memorial Day barbecue only to find them sold-out because these knuckle-headed Nazis are parading for Aryan dignity in a show of solidarity due to a recent rash of Nazi's mouths getting slapped by a rampaging Polack.

They've never entered a record store hoping to purchase the latest Iron Maiden album only to be treated to a two-hour lecture on the ever-evolving musical odyssey of Nick Cave by a fifty year-old Hipster in tight jeans, horned-rim glasses and a mullet.

And, finally, they've never had to dodge Chinese stars while walking to a truck stop for a sixer of Bud Light and a couple scratchers, because Ninjas can't resist fucking with fellas wearing headbands and muscle shirts.

Karl Koweski is a displaced Region Rat now living in rural Alabama. He writes when his pen allows it. He's a husband to a lovely wife and father to some fantastic kids. He collects pop culture ephemera. On most days he prefers Flash Gordon to Luke Skywalker and Neil Diamond to Elvis Presley.

MORE ROADSIDE PRESS TITLES:

Bar Guide for the Seriously Deranged
Alan Catlin

Born on Good Friday
Nathan Graziano

Under Normal Conditions
Karl Koweski

The Dead and the Desperate
Dan Denton

Clown Gravy
Misti Rainwater-Lites

Walking Away
Michael D. Grover

All in a Pretty Little Row
Dan Provost

These Are the People in Your Neighbourhood
Jordan Trethewey

They Said I Wasn't College Material
Scot Young

Radio Water
Francine Witte

And Blackberries Grew Wild
Susan Mickelberry

Licorice Heart
Miles Budimir

MORE ROADSIDE PRESS TITLES:

Maze
Jennifer Juneau

Green Roses Bloom for Icarus
Hiromi Yoshida

Let the Scaffolds Fall
Shaun Rouser

Apocalypsing
Jason Anderson

Failing to Fall
James Griffin

The Things We Tell
Sara Glasser

Last Bacchanale
George Wallace